Murder on the line . . .

"SVU Substance Abuse Hot Line," she repeated. "This is operator number three."

Man, she sounded cool. So cold, butter wouldn't melt in that luscious mouth of hers. But he could tell that it was all an act. He grasped the phone more tightly, ready to give her what she needed. Suddenly he wanted to torment her. Scare her. Break her free from that icy shell. Let her be who she really was deep inside. *Force* her to be—

"Is anyone there? How can I help you?"

A hint of strain, not good. She'd hang up soon, he knew. He'd let her suffer long enough. "Help me?" he began, his voice aching. "Ohhh . . . I can think of a lot of ways."

He heard her sharp intake of breath. Then the line fell silent. But he could tell she hadn't hung up. He licked his dry lips. "How's this for a change?" he asked. "I'm calling to help *you*. And I *can* help you. You do believe me, don't you?"

"H-How can you help me?" she asked nervously.

"I can help you understand. I know you 'cause you're just like me. You're torn in two." He waited and smiled. The very fact that she had stayed on the line told him he was right.

Bantam Books in the Sweet Valley University series.
Ask your bookseller for the books you have missed.

And don't miss these Sweet Valley
University Thriller Editions:

Visit the Official Sweet Valley Web Site on the Internet at:

http://www.sweetvalley.com

SWEET VALLEY UNIVERSITY®

THRILLER EDITION

Don't Answer the Phone

Written by
Laurie John

Created by
FRANCINE PASCAL

BANTAM BOOKS
NEW YORK · TORONTO · LONDON · SYDNEY · AUCKLAND

To Johanna McNelis

RL 8, age 14 and up

DONT ANSWER THE PHONE
A Bantam Book / September 1998

ISBN: 0-553-49226-8

Published simultaneously in the United States and Canada

Bantam Books are published by Bantam Books, a division of Bantam
Doubleday Dell Publishing Group, Inc. Its trademark, consisting of the
words "Bantam Books" and the portrayal of a rooster, is Registered in
U.S. Patent and Trademark Office and in other countries. Marca
Registrada. Bantam Books, 1540 Broadway, New York, New York 10036.

PRINTED IN THE UNITED STATES OF AMERICA

OPM   0 9 8 7 6 5 4 3 2 1

Chapter
One

Noah is going to kill me! Alexandra Rollins thought as she hurried across the quad toward her dorm. For the third time this week she was late to meet her boyfriend—and now she was late on a Saturday night, no less! Ignoring the painful stitch in her side, she dashed across the wide stone steps of the library and ducked into a shortcut between the administration building and the bookstore, both of which were closed and dark.

As the pale pink stucco walls and red-tiled roof of Parker Hall came into view, she checked her watch. Forty-five minutes late! Even worse than the last two times. Pushing her coppery waves out of her face, she raced up the sidewalk and into the dorm's brightly lit entrance lobby. No sign of Noah Pearson anywhere.

"Come on!" Slapping the elevator button in

frustration, she looked at the numbers. Evidently someone was holding the door open up on the sixth floor.

Too impatient to wait another second, she darted into the stairwell. "Noah is a great boyfriend," she reassured herself as she began her climb to the fourth floor. "He'll be cool about this. He'll understand. He always does. I'll call him and explain as soon as I get to my room . . . *if* I ever get to my room," she added, leaning heavily against the railing as she made her way up the last few steps to the fourth-floor landing.

Although the number four was missing from the stairwell door, Alexandra had no doubt she was on the right floor. She could have found it with her eyes closed, as if she'd honed in on home base by sonar. The fourth floor was the noisiest floor in Parker Hall.

The moment she burst from the stairwell into the hallway, her ears were assaulted by the sounds of screams, gunshots, and crashing glass. Alexandra rolled her eyes with disgust. Cheri Beinveni, who lived in the room right next door to Alexandra, was a horror movie fanatic. The eerie sound effects from her beloved teen slasher movies, always played at maximum volume, had become Parker Hall's fourth-floor sound track.

"Turn that thing down!" Alexandra yelled as

she passed Cheri's door—just out of principle. Complaining rarely did any good. As a film student, Cheri considered the daily video blood fests to be her homework. Everyone on the floor had become so desensitized to the sounds of murder and mayhem that Alexandra figured they could all be massacred in their beds and no one would even think for a second that the chaos was real.

Leaning against her own door, she dug to the bottom of her book bag for her keys. Through the flimsy wood she could hear her roommate, Trina Slezniak, talking. *Oh, great, she's on the phone,* Alexandra silently grumbled. How could she call Noah and apologize if Trina was hogging the line?

But as she stepped into the room she realized that wasn't going to be a problem. There was Noah, dressed in his best suit and tie, pacing up and down the narrow space between her bed and Trina's like some caged animal in a zoo.

"Hi, you guys!" Alexandra flashed her most disarming smile. "Wow, Noah, you look handsome tonight." She tossed her book bag onto her desk, yanked open her tiny closet, and began to rummage for her olive green sweater.

"Trina let me in to wait for you," Noah yelled over the rising crescendo of organ music from next door. "I suppose *you* were expecting me to wait downstairs in that dreary, lonely lounge for another hour or so."

Uh-oh, she thought, noting the strain in his usually soft voice. He wasn't just trying to be heard over the next-door noise. No, he was definitely hopping mad.

She glanced in Trina's direction, hoping for some support. Trina simply gave an embarrassed shrug and jumped to her feet.

"I'm gonna go ask Cheri to turn that mess down," Trina mumbled. She skittered out of the room like a scared rabbit and slammed the door behind her.

Alexandra turned back to Noah, a contrite look on her face. "Sorry I'm late, but it was unavoidable."

"It always is lately." The racket from next door stopped suddenly, making Noah's words sound even more harsh and loud.

Alexandra poked a finger in her ear and jiggled it. "Whew! Thank goodness Trina was able to talk some sense into Cheri for once. That horrible noise was about to drive me crazy—and I just got here. I can imagine how you must be feeling."

"Can you?" he asked crossly. "I seriously doubt that."

His tone reminded her that she still owed him a big explanation. "I was at Theta house," she said, pulling out a floral skirt and holding it up to see if it matched the sweater.

"Like I'm surprised!" Noah leaned against the open closet door. Even though he was

4

slightly taller than Alexandra, his position allowed him to stare accusingly at her, eye to eye.

Alexandra looked away. "It was an important meeting. Attendance was mandatory, and I couldn't get away early. The new pledges were being introduced and—"

"Oh, that explains everything!" Noah lifted his hands and dropped them helplessly. "I can easily understand why you forgot about *me*, then. How can a poor guy who is using his one and only day off work to take his girlfriend to a sold-out production of *Phantom of the Opera* possibly compare to a juicy gossip fest about some new sorority sisters?"

"I can't believe it. You're actually jealous."

"No." He took the skirt out of her hands and dropped it over the back of her desk chair. "I'm just fed up, Alex. Theta Alpha Theta is not the beginning and the end of the earth. Contrary to what you might believe, there's a whole world of experience outside that Victorian house of ill manners."

"Ill manners?" She tossed back her hair, stuck out her chin, and met his gaze. "I'll have you know, Thetas have *perfect* manners. We happen to be the most elegant, prestigious sorority on campus—"

"Save it for the pledges, Alex. I'm not interested in hearing your 'Theta-is-the-best' propaganda. It's all you talk about anymore."

He rolled his brown eyes upward. "Sorry, Noah," he mocked in a prissy falsetto, "I can't have dinner with you this evening. It's noodle night at the sorority house."

"Pasta night, Noah. It's pasta night."

He held out a limp-wristed arm and cocked his hip to one side. "Sorry, Noah, I can't meet you at the Red Lion. Alison and the girls think coffeehouses are tacky. Not the right *image* for a Theta!"

"So you suddenly hate sororities?"

He scowled. "No, I don't hate them at all," he replied in his natural voice. "I think sororities are fine for meeting people and making friends. They're great for creating a homey atmosphere and sense of belonging for kids far away from home for the first time. But they aren't the be-all and end-all of existence. If you were doing something worthwhile with your sorority, I might overlook being ignored . . . *occasionally*. But really, Alex—teas? You spend all your time at initiations, dinner parties, fashion shows, and . . . and . . . nail-painting marathons." He wiggled his fingers in her face. "Everything they do is shallow and superficial. I hate to say it, but you're becoming more like Jessica Wakefield every day."

Alexandra chose to ignore that remark. Jessica was the identical twin of her ex–best friend, Elizabeth Wakefield. And except for being Thetas at Sweet Valley University and having gone to the same high school, she and Jessica had nothing in common— absolutely nothing. Biting the inside of her cheek to keep from screaming, she slammed the closet door and yanked the skirt off the back of the chair.

Get dressed, Alexandra, she silently commanded herself. *Don't let Noah snare you into his gripey mood. He'll cool down soon, and everything will be OK.*

"Don't pretend you're the one who's being mistreated here," Noah warned.

Turning her back on him, she stepped on the heels of her tennis shoes and slipped them off, not bothering to untie the laces. Without a word she padded silently across the floor in her socks.

Noah followed right behind her, lecturing the whole time about how her friends were corrupting her. He was so close that when she stopped suddenly, he crashed right into her.

"I'm going out to the bathroom to change clothes," she announced in a steely voice. "Are you planning to follow me?"

He backed off a step and ran his hands through his shaggy, dark blond hair. "Don't bother changing."

"Noah, it won't take me three minutes."

"It's too late, Alex. This whole night is already ruined. Even if we left right now, we'd still miss the first act! *Phantom of the Opera* has been the school's biggest production of the year, and tonight is the last night. You knew how much trouble I had getting these tickets—not to mention how much they cost me."

7

"Sor-ry," she said with a huff. "I'll pay you for the stupid tickets."

"See, that's exactly what I'm talking about!" Noah yanked his tie loose and unbuttoned his top button as if his shirt were choking him. "I'm not worried about the money—even though I did have to scrounge around for weeks to save up enough. What I'm worried about is your *attitude*. I went to all this trouble, taking off work, planning this great date for you, but apparently you don't even care."

She opened her mouth to protest.

"Alex, I'm carrying a full load of classes," Noah interrupted. "I'm holding down two part-time jobs, and on top of that I'm putting in hours as a volunteer in the psych lab. All in all, I'd say I'm a pretty busy guy. But have you ever noticed that I still make time for you? I still call and come over and take you out. *And,* I might add, somehow I always manage to be on *time!*"

Alexandra stared in amazement. She'd never seen Noah so riled up. Normally he was the epitome of patience and understanding. "Noah, I think you're overreacting."

"No. I'm not. I think *you've* forgotten what's important in life."

"And what's that? You?"

"I'd like to think so every once in a while!"

"You are not the only person on this campus,

Noah Pearson! Do you think I don't have a social life outside of you?"

"I know you do. That's the problem. Your *whole* social life is apparently outside of me!" Noah shrugged. "I thought you and I were supposed to be each other's top priority. But I guess I've just been kidding myself. Evidently I'm *way* down on your list. When do I get a little attention, Alex?"

She glared at her boyfriend. This was so unlike Noah; she'd never seen him so clingy and possessive. "Back off a little, OK? You're smothering me." She turned away and reached for the doorknob.

"Alexandra."

When she looked back at Noah and saw the unspilled tears glistening in his eyes, she immediately regretted her shrewish tone. *Poor Noah,* she thought. He had been working really hard. She'd been telling him for ages that he was overdoing it. He looked like he was practically exhausted. The pressure of having to pay for school and keep his grades up was obviously starting to get to him.

Alexandra hadn't meant to hurt him. Really, she had to admit to herself, he had every right to be annoyed. She was the one who had spoiled their evening by being late—although she still didn't see it as the outrageous crime he was making it out to be.

Swallowing back her annoyance, she reached

out for him. "I'm sorry, sweetie. I know I probably haven't been the best girlfriend lately. And I shouldn't have been late tonight. I'll try to make it up to you." She leaned toward him and draped her arms over his shoulders. With a forgiving smile, she twined her fingers together behind his head and pulled him toward her. But to her surprise, Noah stiffly ducked out from under her arms and pulled away.

After she left, Noah flopped down on Alexandra's narrow bed and crossed his arms over his chest. He'd thought Alexandra was a caring, sensitive, mature woman, but evidently he'd been wrong. Either that or that stupid sorority of hers had brainwashed every last drop of decency out of her. One of the first things that had attracted him to Alexandra had been her sense of independence—and now it was gone.

I should have seen it coming, he thought, directing some of his anger back at himself. She'd been changing for weeks, but now she'd apparently reached the point of no return. She was becoming nothing but a flighty sorority babe—a Jessica Wakefield clone whose social world was the only important thing in her life.

"Oh, Alex, where are you?" He groaned, blinking away the tears that welled up in his eyes. "Where's the girl I fell in love with?"

"Ta-da," she sang, coming back into the room as if on cue. She twirled around and struck a pose. "See? In the bathroom and out in two shakes. I'm ready in record time."

Noah sat up and stared at the gorgeous copper-haired creature in the clingy green sweater and flowing skirt as if she were a stranger.

After a moment Alexandra frowned and threw up her hands in an exasperated gesture. "You look very nice, Alexandra!" she said, prompting him.

I'm not going to do it, he told himself. *I'm not going to look into that beautiful face and give in the way I always do.* But he looked. Her sparkling eyes—so much greener tonight because of her sweater—seemed to be drawing him into their spell.

No! he thought, stiffening his spine. *Why do I always have to be the one to apologize? Not this time. This time I'm way too mad.*

He stood up and looked her right in her big green eyes. "I know this is going to come as a big surprise to you, Alexandra. But contrary to what Theta Alpha Theta teaches, the perfect outfit does *not* cure all the world's problems."

She rolled her eyes. "Come on, Noah. Let's go salvage what we can of our night. At least we can see the last half of *Phantom*. After all, the tickets are already paid for."

With shaking fingers he pulled out his wallet and fished the two folded tickets from the center pocket.

11

He tossed them onto the bed. "Here. You go if you want, but count me out. I'm tired of this."

"Noah!"

"You're becoming a sorority robot," he continued, undaunted. "The Thetas have you programmed to forget friends, family, and loved ones. All they care about is that you have the right look and that you're at the right party with the right people. They won't tolerate any deviance from the mold. I wouldn't be surprised if those sorority snobs order you to dump me and start dating a Sigma—if they haven't already."

"You're being ridiculous."

"No, I'm not. And maybe they're right. Maybe you ought to start shopping around for a Sigma or at least a Zeta. I *know* you like *jocks!*" he spat. Just that tiny reminder of her old boyfriend, Mark Gathers, caused him to clench his jaw to the aching point. "I don't know how I can continue to date someone who has no sense of responsibility."

"What do you mean by that?"

"Alex, you've been late the last three times you were supposed to meet me."

"I know, but—"

"But nothing. Every time your excuse has been something frivolous."

"Frivolous?" she parroted.

"Sorority, shopping, getting your hair colored—"

"Highlighted."

"Whatever. But you always have some dumb excuse."

Alexandra threw up her hands. "Have you ever thought that maybe all those things are important to me?"

"That's what scares me. What's happening, Alex? You're changing."

"Darn right I'm changing."

"I don't even know who you are anymore."

"Well, I'll tell you who I'm *not!*" Angrily she yanked open the top drawer of her desk and shuffled around in a box of photos until she found one. Dangling a school photo in front of his face, she shouted, "There! Do you recognize that mousy girl?"

Noah tilted his head back a bit and squinted. "Of course—"

"Don't you dare say it's me, because it isn't! It's *Enid*, Noah. Enid Rollins. That pathetic little creature was the most boring, invisible girl ever to pass through the halls of Sweet Valley High."

Noah took the photo from her fingers and studied it. The girl in the photo was slightly plumper. Her hair was a little darker red and a little more frizzy than the glossy highlighted waves Alexandra wore now. But it was clearly Alexandra. When he opened his mouth to say so, she practically jumped down his throat.

13

"Enid Rollins was the girl I *used* to be," she railed. "Enid was a nobody. She had no life of her own—just the scraps left over from Elizabeth Wakefield's life. She did what everyone expected her to do. She never broke a rule. Never took a stand. She studied hard; said, 'yes, ma'am,' 'please,' and 'thank you'; and never, *ever* cut in line. She was afraid to take risks . . . or to live."

"Well, I'll bet she would at least have shown up on time for her dates," Noah snarled.

Alexandra snatched the picture from his fingers and ripped it in half. "I'll never be that girl again, Noah. Never!"

"Maybe I'm missing something here, but I don't see what the big horror is. Enid doesn't sound all that bad to me. In fact, I think I might have liked her. I'll bet she would have treated her boyfriend with the respect he deserved."

Alexandra stuck her arms straight down at her sides and clenched her hands into tight fists. "Yes, she probably would have. And no doubt she'd have been *so* grateful to have a handsome, sexy boyfriend, she'd have let him walk all over her in the process. But not me! I love you, Noah. But if Enid is what you want, then you might as well leave right now because I laid that mousy little creature in the grave the moment I set foot on campus." She pointed a shaky finger at the door.

Noah paused, one hand on the doorknob, and

14

looked back at her. "OK, Alex, I'm going, but let me remind you of one thing. A person doesn't just put on an identity like a mask. You can't go to your bag of names and say, 'Today I'm going to be Alexandra.' It's fine for people to grow and change, but we're always shaped by our past. If Enid is who you were in high school, then she's still a part of you. And if you hate Enid, that means you hate a part of yourself."

Alexandra turned her back to him, but he knew she was still listening. "Alex, if you can't love yourself completely, how can you expect to love anyone else? How can you love *me*?"

Chapter Two

"I think the monthly Sunday morning brunch is a great tradition, don't you?" Alexandra asked as she and two of her sorority sisters, Jessica Wakefield and Lila Fowler, walked down Cherry Street toward the main part of the campus.

"I'd like it a lot better if we didn't have to have it so *early*," Jessica complained with a toss of her golden hair. "I had to get up practically before the sun!"

"That's just because it takes you so long to get beautiful," Lila teased.

Jessica squealed indignantly, and they all laughed.

Alexandra knew it was teasing; Lila and Jessica considered their daily beauty ritual a sacred thing. Both were the type who'd wear makeup and designer clothes to a mud-wrestling contest.

"Speaking of beauty," Jessica said. "How do you like this new lavender cashmere sweater?" She ran her hand down her sleeve and smiled.

"I think it's gorgeous," Alexandra said. "And those amethyst earrings really set it off."

"The earrings are mine," Lila added importantly. "But the sweater is to die for, Jess. Is that the one you got at Mais Oui's big sale last week?"

Jessica nodded.

As Lila and Jessica launched into a discussion of their favorite shopping venues Alexandra tuned them out. She looked around the nearly deserted campus in disappointment. Here she was, walking down the sidewalk with two of the most beautiful, popular girls at Sweet Valley University, and there was nobody around to appreciate it—not anyone that she knew anyway.

Imagine what those snobs from high school would think if they could see me now! she thought gleefully. Jessica and Lila had been two of those snobs; back at Sweet Valley High, they'd rarely given old Enid the time of day. Now Enid had become Alexandra, and she had become part of the in crowd—she was *accepted*. "Accepted" was *not* the kind of word anyone would have attached to Enid Rollins. If any of the "kids back home," as she liked to think of them, had a chance to see her walking through campus as thick as thieves with two of the most popular and beautiful girls from SVH, they wouldn't believe their eyes.

She knew it seemed a little shallow, but her

17

association with her popular sorority sisters was important to her. Not only was it fun, but it was proof she'd changed. Just before she'd packed up and moved off to Sweet Valley University, she'd realized that being in a whole new environment would give her a chance to become a whole new person. That was why she'd decided to put her Enid persona aside and go by her middle name, Alexandra. With her past behind her she could become the young woman she'd always wanted to be—slimmer, prettier, more popular. It had worked. Mousy, good-little-girl Enid was gone forever.

But why am I thinking about high-school days? Enid thought. *Ugh!* Just dragging out that awful picture last night had been enough to make the dowdy image of Enid stick in her mind and bring her self-confidence crashing down.

"Alex, how did you like SVU's production of *Phantom* last night?" Lila asked as they passed the theater. "Didn't you think it was every bit as good as the Broadway version?"

"I didn't see it," Alexandra said. "Noah was angry because I was a little late. So we didn't go."

"Noah Pearson angry? *That* I'd like to see," Jessica said in disbelief.

No, you wouldn't! Alexandra thought, remembering the look of disgust Noah had given her last night as he'd shrugged off her embrace.

"Didn't you tell him we had a sorority meeting?" Lila asked.

"Yes, but he—"

"Well, that's what you get for dating a guy who isn't in a fraternity," Jessica said indignantly. "They just don't understand. I know when I was dating—"

"Oh no," Lila interrupted, sticking her palm into Jessica's face. "Don't go there, Jess. We don't have the time or the energy to get into the details of your love life."

Alexandra was almost relieved when Jessica and Lila began to argue about whose boyfriend history was the most disastrous. At least it moved the conversation away from Noah. And right now the less she thought about him, the better.

"Here's my stop," Alexandra said, pausing in front of the psychology building.

"You don't really want to work, do you?" Jessica moaned. "Why don't you come with us? Lila and I are going to her room to coordinate our outfits for the big-sister ceremony Wednesday afternoon." Jessica didn't talk as much as she bubbled. Everything about her was bright and sparkling.

"Thanks, Jess," Alexandra said, not bothering to hide her disappointment. "But I really can't. It's my day to open up." She dangled the keys and nodded toward the unobtrusive side door that led to the SVU Substance Abuse Hot Line's two-room office.

"Ah, come on," Lila urged. "Surely they don't expect any crazies to call on Sunday morning. Anybody with any sense is sleeping. I know that's where I'd be if we hadn't had that pledge brunch!"

"But don't you see?" Jessica explained with a giggle. "They're druggies. They don't *have* any sense. That's why they're calling the hot line."

Alexandra glanced around in embarrassment. Jessica's voice was loud enough to be heard several feet away.

"C'mon, Alex, what do you say?" Jessica continued, obviously fighting to hold back her laughter. "Flip on the answering machine and let the losers talk to themselves."

"Or hook them to a conference call and let them talk to one another," Lila suggested.

"Right, they'd never know the difference," Jessica insisted. "They're going to tell all their troubles to strangers anyway."

Jessica and Lila slapped their palms together. Alexandra joined in their laughter, although she didn't think their comments had been all that funny. She felt pretty guilty about not sticking up for the hot line or for the callers who needed the service, but she knew it was *not* the kind of thing Jessica or Lila would have understood.

20

"So are you gonna stay here and talk to a bunch of social rejects or come with us for a lesson in fashion sense?" Jessica asked, striking her best modeling pose.

Alexandra sighed. "I wish I could go with you, but duty calls. And I'd better get a move on. I'm late."

"Want us to come inside with you?" Lila asked.

"Lila!" Jessica cried out in her most appalled voice. "You don't think *I'm* going to talk to any of those weirdos, do you?"

"No, I just thought maybe Alexandra would like to have us around till she gets everything set up. Don't you feel creepy in that big old building, all alone?" Lila asked.

"No, it's no big deal," Alexandra said with a shrug. "I'll be fine. Thanks anyway."

After her friends walked away, Alexandra slipped into the outer office of the Substance Abuse Hot Line and flipped the light switch. Hesitantly the old fluorescent tubes hummed to life overhead.

Contrary to what she'd told Lila and Jessica, it sometimes *did* bother her to be the only person in the whole building. But there really wasn't much she could do about it. The Substance Abuse Hot Line staff had dwindled lately, and rarely did they have enough volunteers to open all three lines at once. Saturdays and Sundays were especially bad because no one wanted to work the weekends—and strangely enough, despite Lila and Jessica's joking, Sundays were actually heavy call-in days. Many substance abusers tended to feel guilty or repentant after their weekend—especially alcohol abusers. Alexandra knew that from personal experience. . . .

After adjusting the thermostat she turned on the lights in the back room, pulled her paperback—*The Letters of Abelard and Heloise,* for her medieval history class—from her purse, and tucked her purse under her chair. She was operating on automatic. Her thoughts were still on her sorority sisters. She could hardly believe that she had just turned down an invitation to pal around with Jessica Wakefield and Lila Fowler. In fact, Alexandra could hardly believe she'd just been *asked* to pal around with them. Back in high school Jessica would rather have dined on garden slugs than be seen in the company of "drippy ol' Enid"—not exactly a term that endeared her to Alexandra.

There was certainly no love lost on Enid's part either. She had detested Jessica when she was in high school—absolutely hated her. It was only after she'd matured and was able to distance herself from her Enid persona that she'd realized most of her old feelings about Jessica had stemmed from jealousy. Deep down, she'd always known Jessica was the person she wanted to be. Free, fun loving, exuberant, pretty, and popular— maybe Alexandra still had a ways to go, but she was getting there.

Suddenly the phone rang, causing her to jump. It was quickly followed by a click, a beep, and then hot line volunteer Cindy Lee's well-modulated voice. "You have reached the SVU Substance Abuse Hot Line. There is no one available to take your call at the moment. Please try again later. The hot line is open daily from . . ."

Alexandra scrambled for her receiver, but the caller had already hung up.

Now Alexandra felt doubly guilty—guilty that she'd stood by and let her friends make fun of the hot line and guilty that she'd been so busy day-dreaming about them that she hadn't opened the lines in time to catch a caller. The hot line meant a lot to her. She didn't want to mess this job up.

With a sigh she opened the phone line to cubicle number three and picked up her paperback. But she'd hardly had time to find her place before the phone rang again.

"Hello, SVU Substance Abuse Hot Line," she said. "How are you today?"

Immediately a young woman who was trying to give up smoking launched into a long-winded story about how if she didn't get a cigarette soon, she was afraid she was going to climb the bell tower in the quad and start shooting people.

"How long have you made it without a ciga-rette?" Alexandra asked.

"Twenty-eight hours and . . . thirty-four min-utes. If you count the time I was asleep."

"That's a pretty good start."

"But I'm afraid it's about to be the end. I'm dying here. My hands are shaking and I . . . See, I've been smoking since I was thirteen."

"What made you decide to stop?"

"Huh?"

"I said, what—"

"I heard what you said. I'm just surprised. I figured you'd probably preach at me or some-thing."

Alexandra smiled. "No. I'm just here to listen, mostly. Anyway, I'll bet you get enough preaching from other people."

"Are you kidding? My mother. My roommate. Now my boyfriend is getting in on the act. He's started the bit about, 'We love you and we want you around for a long, long time. . . .' You know, the whole health thing."

"So you're quitting for your boyfriend?"

"No. It's kinda funny, I guess. But this week-end I just decided I wanted to give it up. For me."

"Good for you. Say, you don't have to give me your real name, but do you have a name I could call you for now?"

The caller paused. "Winona."

Alexandra smiled again. "OK, Winona. If you really want to quit smoking, then go ahead and do it. Nothing's stopping you."

"I know, I'm trying. But it's my hands. They don't know I've quit. Every time I turn around, I'm reaching for a cigarette. I don't even know it till I'm poking it in my mouth."

"Do you have a pack in your dorm room right now?" Alexandra asked, already knowing the answer. Even when things were at their worst, Alexandra could hardly bring herself to pour her last bottle of vodka down the drain. It had seemed like such a waste. . . .

"Y-Yes. Three packs, actually."

"Get rid of them," Alexandra instructed. "Throw them out, give them away, whatever. You shouldn't have that temptation so close to you, Winona. And throwing them out will be your next big step toward quitting. If you have the strength to do that, you'll realize you have the strength to keep going."

After a long pause the caller said, "OK."

"Good. Now, what's the worst thing you could do right now?"

"You mean besides climbing up the bell tower?"

"Yes," Alexandra said with a chuckle. "Besides that."

"Smoke a cigarette?" The caller sounded unsure that she was giving the right answer.

"What would happen if you do?"

"Well . . . then I guess . . . I fail. It means I can't quit."

"No. It just means that you'd have to start all over again and see if next time you can go twenty-*nine* hours."

"You know what? You're right. But I'm only about twenty minutes from that right now. I think I can make it."

"Great," Alexandra said. "Maybe you can even round it off to thirty hours."

"Maybe so."

"If you think it'd help to talk to other people who are trying to give up smoking, I can give you the number of a group here on campus that meets once a week." Alexandra flipped through the sheaf of papers tacked to the bulletin board behind her and read off a number.

"Thanks," the caller said gratefully. "You've been a big help."

"Listen, Winona, call me back when you make it to the thirty-hour mark."

"Really? Are you serious? Call back today, you mean?"

"Sure. I'll be here."

"But what if I—"

"Change is hard. But we can do it if we really

want to badly enough. I'll be looking for your call in about an hour and twenty minutes. OK? Just ask for operator number three." Alexandra didn't like to give the impression she was the only one working the phones. "Take care, Winona."

"OK. You too, Number Three."

After the caller hung up, Alexandra nodded. *Good job,* she told herself. She loved the feeling of immense satisfaction that came whenever she was able to help a caller.

Once upon a time, she would have had a serious problem with accepting compliments, even from herself—but no longer. If she'd learned anything since coming to college, it was that she had to like herself before others could like her.

Her smile faded as she was suddenly reminded of Noah's parting words. The nerve of him, saying that she hated a part of herself because she hated Enid! That was utterly ridiculous. She wasn't Enid. Enid Rollins no longer existed. Hadn't she just proved it? Enid could never have talked to that smoker the way Alexandra had—that was for sure. That pathetic creature could never have talked to *anyone* with that much confidence or conviction.

Enid! Just the very name made her stomach boil. That poor girl—always tagging along in Elizabeth Wakefield's shadow—was a nobody who deserved to die. How dare Noah suggest that he'd have been happier with that dishrag!

"Well, let me tell you, Noah Pearson," she muttered, "just because I laid Enid to rest does *not* mean I hate a part of myself. Enid isn't a part of me. Not anymore."

Even though Noah wasn't present, it made her feel better to say all the things she should have said last night. She was still rattling them off when the phone's ring interrupted her. She temporarily shoved aside her anger at Noah and picked up the phone.

"Hello, SVU Substance Abuse Hot Line," she answered in her cheeriest, most helpful voice.

"Hello?" a soft, almost whispery male voice said—no, *asked*—as it came timidly across the line.

"Hot line," Alexandra repeated. "How can I help?"

"I—I . . . well, see . . . I . . ." The caller paused. Alexandra could hear him breathing.

"Nothing you say is being recorded in any way," Alexandra informed him. "I can assure you that every call to the hot line is kept strictly confidential."

The caller cleared his throat. "Well, I—I used to be sort of . . . a heavy drinker. I quit . . . but now I really, really want a drink."

Alexandra's heart went out to the caller immediately. She too had had a problem with alcohol since coming to college. Right after her first college boyfriend, Mark Gathers, had left school and dumped her, Alexandra had been so miserable she'd turned to alcohol to escape from her problems. She could totally relate.

"Do you mean you'd like a drink right this minute?" she asked.

"Yes. I know that sounds crazy. Here it is, hardly past noon on a Sunday . . ." The caller's voice ebbed away.

"Are you still there?" she said calmly into the silent receiver.

"Yes. I—I know I should be ashamed—"

"No, you don't have to feel ashamed. Listen, you don't have to tell me who you are, but do you have a name I could call you for now?"

"Uh . . . Rodin."

"Rodan? Like from the Godzilla movies?" Alexandra asked, smiling.

"No. The sculptor . . . you know, *The Thinker*?"

Ah, the quiet, artsy type, Alexandra thought. "OK, listen, Rodin. Don't be so hard on yourself. You've quit once before, so you know alcohol cravings don't exactly go by the clock. When they come, they come. And the only thing you can do is try to deal with it. But craving alcohol doesn't mean you're a bad person."

"I feel like it does, though."

"Trust me. It doesn't. Why do you think you want a drink right now?"

"I—I don't know. I just do."

"Is something bothering you that you'd like to talk about?"

"No. Well . . . yes. It's really no big deal, but . . . I guess it's just loneliness. See, I'm kinda shy, and I just started here this semester. I don't have any friends."

"Give yourself time. I'm sure you'll have some friends soon."

"Maybe. But—"

"Can I make a suggestion?"

"Sure."

"Next time you feel like crawling into a bottle, go out somewhere—someplace where other students are hanging out. And I don't mean a frat party."

"How about a bar?" he asked, his tone lighter. The very fact that he seemed to feel comfortable enough to joke with her was a good sign.

"Better avoid the bar, I think. Go to the coffee shop, or the bookstore, or . . . even the laundry room. Do you live in a dorm, Rodin?"

"Uh . . . yeah."

"Try this the next time you feel lonely. Go to the TV lounge and make yourself speak to at least one person."

"You don't know these guys. It's so hard. . . ."

"I know it is. But would you at least try it? If that doesn't help, then you can call me back here at the hot line—"

"You wouldn't mind if I called you back? I mean, you . . . how would I . . . who would I . . . I don't even know your name."

"Just ask for operator number three. Even if you happen to call when I'm not here, someone else will be here. We're here to listen, Rodin. And understand."

"OK. Thanks. I feel better. I guess I just needed to know that someone out there understood how I feel."

"Believe me, I do."

"Thanks again. You've been a big help."

"I'm glad."

Alexandra hung up, feeling entirely satisfied. *I helped him,* she thought. She leaned back in her chair and stretched her tired back.

"A little applause, please," she murmured. She clapped and cheered quietly, feeling a little silly. "Well, if I don't pat myself on the back, who will?" she asked the empty office. "Not Noah, that's for sure."

She glowered as thoughts of Noah returned. She had met Noah in psychology class, but she had fallen in love with him over the hot line. It wasn't because they were working together. No, Noah had been the guy she'd called when she'd hit rock bottom. He had been the one who'd picked up the phone when she'd called the hot line to admit she was an alcoholic. "T Squared,"

31

he'd named himself. And her pseudonym had been . . . Enid.

She took out her compact and dusted a little powder over her freckles. The face in the mirror was exactly who she wanted to be. "This is who I am," she said aloud. "I am Alexandra Rollins. I help others." She snapped the compact closed and shoved it into her purse. "How can Noah not recognize that?"

Chapter Three

Luke Winterson dug his thumbs into the lump of clay on the table in front of him and smiled. He loved Mondays. There was no better way to start the week than by coming to sculpture class. Not only because he loved to sculpt—which he did—but mostly because from where he sat, he had a perfect view of Alexandra Rollins.

She was so beautiful, she took his breath away. He'd had a crush on her since the first day of class. When she walked into the sculpture studio, all the brightly colored artwork in the room had paled by comparison.

Out of the corner of his eye he watched as she concentrated on the whirling lump of clay on the pottery wheel between her knees. She wasn't looking his way, so he moved into a position where he could watch her more openly. He adored the tiny wrinkles of concentration right in the middle of her forehead.

Luke ached to capture that face on canvas. Maybe someday she would model for him. Her thick bouncy waves formed a coppery halo around a face like an angel's. Her long dark lashes practically rested on her creamy cheeks as she looked down at the lopsided bowl she was forming. Her hands moved up and down the wet clay seductively. It reminded him of a really sexy scene he'd seen in a movie once. Suddenly embarrassed, he shifted back to the other side of his table.

"She's out of your league, Luke old boy," he whispered to the self-portrait bust he was making. He'd been telling himself those same words since that first day of Sculpture 101—the day she'd stolen his heart. She was a beautiful sorority girl. He could tell at a glance that she was popular, stylish, and elegant. Someone like her would never be interested in anyone as dull, shy, and mild mannered as he was. It was one of the sad facts of life, but it didn't stop him from dreaming. Luke sighed. If only he had the guts to talk to her—

In person, that is, he amended silently. Just remembering how her voice had sounded over the phone yesterday made him ache all over.

How lucky could I get? he asked himself, remembering how he'd just happened to see her crossing campus yesterday morning with two other sorority girls. He hadn't meant to eavesdrop, but they'd passed right by him, laughing and talking so loudly, he couldn't help it.

At first they'd sounded so stuck-up and superior, his heart had sunk with disappointment. But when he saw her part company and go into the little door marked SVU Substance Abuse Hot Line, he realized there was still hope. If a woman as beautiful and popular as Alexandra could give up her free time to help people in need, there was obviously more to her than met the eye. He knew right then that he had to call her. He just had to hear her voice and take a chance on getting to know her a little bit.

He bumped his glasses back up his nose with his wrist and smiled, remembering her voice. He'd known it was her from her first hello. And what's more, he could tell just by the sound of her voice that she wasn't stuck-up or shallow. She was just the way he'd imagined in his daydreams: mature, patient, caring, sympathetic, and understanding.

That was when he knew that what he'd been feeling was more than mere infatuation . . . much more than just physical attraction. He was in love with Alexandra Rollins—totally, completely, head over heels in love.

He glanced back over at her again. *So beautiful,* he mused. *And she's interested in art too. Why else would she still be here working twenty minutes after class ended?*

The two of them were the only ones left in the room. Maybe this was his chance to talk to her—face-to-face.

He laid a moist towel over his sculpture and returned it to the shelf in the back of the studio. On his way back he took the long way around the room so he could pass right by Alexandra.

"Hi," he said with as much nerve as he could muster. "You're Alexandra, aren't you? I'm Luke."

"Nice to meet you, Luke," she said with a polite smile.

When she didn't seem to recognize his voice, he relaxed a little. "Nice bowl."

"Thanks." She gave him another crooked little smile. "It was supposed to be a vase, but I guess it does look more like a bowl, doesn't it?"

Luke felt his cheeks grow warm and knew he was blushing. "You shouldn't have told me," he said lightly, willing his face to stop flushing. "I'd have thought you were an expert at bowl making."

"Did I say vase? Silly me. Of course this is a bowl. What else could it possibly be?" She flicked a strand of hair away from her face, leaving a gray streak on her cheek. Luke wanted to wipe it away, but he didn't dare.

"You have, uh . . ." He touched his own cheek

with a finger. "Clay on your, uh . . . cheek."

She smiled and swiped at her cheek with the back of her hand. "I guess we have a lot in common, then."

"Pardon?"

"We are a matched set," she explained. "You have clay all over your glasses."

Luke pulled his wire-rimmed glasses from his nose. "So I do. No wonder the world has been looking a little gray to me lately."

Her laugh sounded like the song of an angel. "I have tissues in my purse if you want to clean them off."

"That's OK." He folded the bows down and stuck the glasses in his shirt pocket. "I'll clean them up when I get back to the dorm. I only wear them for close work anyway. Eyestrain." He shrugged. "I was having headaches last year, and my mother thought reading glasses might be the answer."

"Did they help?"

"I guess." He looked at his watch. "It's twelve-twenty, and I haven't had a headache in . . . oh, an hour or two," he joked.

Alexandra paled. "Oh no! It can't be that late! I was supposed to meet someone at twelve." She shook a glob of wet clay from her hands. "And now it's going to take me at least fifteen more minutes to clean up this mess. Oh, jeez . . ."

"Don't worry about it. I'll take care of it," Luke offered.

Her green eyes widened and shone with gratitude. Luke felt as if he would pass out right then and there.

"Are you sure you wouldn't mind?" She jumped up and grabbed a handful of paper towels. "I wouldn't normally impose like this, but Noah is going to be furious with me." She turned on the faucet with her elbow, and water rattled into the deep stainless-steel sink. She began cleaning off her arms. "You're a lifesaver, Luke. I thank you, and my boyfriend thanks you."

Luke's heart sank. *Of course someone as lovely as Alexandra would have a boyfriend,* he thought dejectedly. *I wonder if the guy realizes how lucky he is?*

Alexandra dried her arms. "Bye, Luke," she said as she hurried across the studio. "Thanks again for the help."

Feeling forgotten, Luke turned to the pottery wheel. *I just hope the guy treats her with the love and understanding she deserves,* he thought as he began cleaning up the mess. *I know I would.*

With his elbow on the table and his chin in his hand, Noah leaned forward and stared at the slowly congealing food in front of him. His bowl of cafeteria chili—not *that* appetizing when it was hot—was now coated with a thickening orangy red film of grease.

He picked up a spoon with his free hand and savagely stabbed the surface of the chili. The spoon stood upright on its own for several seconds before falling over with a clang.

Noah craned his neck around to look at the clock again. Twelve-thirty. Alexandra was thirty minutes late. Maybe she was trying to beat Saturday night's record.

He picked up a cracker and chomped down on it. *Stale!* he thought, grabbing for his drink to wash it down. But the ice had melted in his glass, turning his cola the unappetizing color of weak tea. He slammed it down on the table angrily.

Why did I even bother calling her? he wondered. The answer wasn't hard to come up with. He'd called Alexandra on Sunday night and apologized because he was missing her like crazy. As exasperating as she could be, he loved her like he'd never loved anyone in his whole life. Once again he'd swallowed his pride, admitted his wrongdoing, and apologized for losing his temper. It had worked—or so he'd thought. They'd made up over the phone and agreed to meet for lunch today.

But now it was clear nothing had changed. She was late again. There was probably an eyelash-curling marathon over at Theta house—another good reason to forget all about him, of course. He picked up his napkin and sandwich and threw them furiously atop the chili bowl. "I'm outta here," he grumbled.

"Noah, wait!"

Noah looked up, a strange combination of relief and disappointment stirring in his chest. Alexandra was winding her way across the crowded cafeteria.

Breathlessly she slid into the chair opposite him. "I'm sorry I'm late," she panted. "Please, sit back down and give me a chance to explain."

He sank back into the chair, but he wasn't listening. Why bother? Whatever words she used were all going to boil down to the fact that he wasn't important enough in her life, wasn't worth showing up on time for, wasn't worth her time at all.

She took a deep breath—to further convince him she'd been rushing, he supposed—and began her excuse. "I've been in art class. I was working on a piece of pottery and didn't finish by the time class ended, so I had to stay. You know how hard that stuff gets if you let it set."

"Pottery! That's just great. First I wasn't as important as your class work. Then I slipped to third behind the sorority. Now I'm losing out to your *hobbies*. Do you have any idea how that makes me feel, Alex?"

"No. How?" Alexandra snapped. "Like a spoiled, possessive, clinging male chauvinist?"

"Very funny. Are you going to take a comedy class next?"

"Get a grip, Noah. Everything isn't about you—"

"No, it's not about me," he interrupted. "It's about you. You and your lack of responsibility. You, constantly making promises you can't keep. You'd rather waste your time making some dumb ashtray than keep a promise."

"For your information, it was a *bowl*, not an ashtray. And what makes you so sure it's a waste of time? Art doesn't have to be just a hobby. Maybe I've decided to major in it."

"Last I heard, you hadn't made up your mind to major in anything. First it was 'maybe history or math.' Last month it was 'maybe English or philosophy.' Now you're saying 'maybe art.' You don't have any idea what you want."

"Yes, I do. What I really want right now is a boyfriend who'll try to understand me. One who will support *my* needs as well as his own."

"In what? I don't even know who you *are* anymore, much less what you think you need."

"Then maybe you should try listening to me once in a while instead of always lecturing." Her green eyes flashed with anger. "I'm a person with many dimensions, Noah. And if you want to keep dating me, you'll have to respect that. I have to be who I am, not who you want me to be. If I expect to become a well-rounded person, I have to try new things." Alexandra leaned forward on her elbows as if she were about to impart some deep, dark secret. "Do you know I was afraid to take this sculpture class at first? Well, I was. I was afraid I wouldn't be good enough. I was afraid I'd fail."

"OK, so you're taking it now. Make all the bowls you want—I'm sure you'll do just great."

"Noah! How dare you—"

"What do you want me to say?" he asked hotly. "That you're brave and daring for playing around with lumps of clay?"

Alexandra backed away and stiffened. "Ever heard of the term liberal arts—as in SVU is a *liberal arts* college? We're supposed to be broadening our horizons here. Developing our intellect and getting a general well-rounded education. Why shouldn't I try all kinds of things? How else am I supposed to know what will make me happy?"

"I thought *I* made you happy . . . but I guess I was wrong." Noah paused to give her an opportunity to protest. But Alexandra didn't. She only sat there fuming.

He licked his lips and reached for the watery soda. At least it was wet enough to wash down the lump that had lodged in his throat. "Alex," he began again after a gulp, "for you to keep searching for something to make you happy when I'm right here makes me feel like I'm doing something wrong. What have I done? Why aren't I enough anymore?"

"Two people can't be *everything* to each other." She looked at him pleadingly, as if she were begging him to see things her way. "Admit it, Noah, we'd be pretty dull people if we had no other outside interests, wouldn't we?"

"You're missing the point," he argued.

"No. *You're* missing the point. There's no use discussing this if your mind is closed." Alexandra jumped up from the chair. "Don't call me again until you feel civil enough to listen for a change." With a haughty toss of her hair she flounced away, leaving Noah so furious, he could hardly move.

"Fine!" he snarled as feeling returned to his numb body. He gathered up his tray, mumbling over it as if Alexandra could hear his every word. "You can bet your pretty little pout I won't be calling anytime soon. This is the last straw! I apologized once, but not again. It's about time for you to realize that you've got everything you need to be happy right now—right here!"

He shoved his tray onto the conveyor belt. *But she won't,* he thought. *Not stubborn Alexandra. She won't realize she's got happiness in the palm of her hand until it's too late—not until it's gone. Forever.*

* * *

How dare Noah Pearson think he knows what I need and don't need, Alexandra fumed as she stormed across the quad. *Just because we're in love doesn't mean he has the right to control me.* The nerve of him, trying to inhibit her personal growth! After all, what was college for if not to experiment and try new things? If he wanted her to stop learning and exploring right now, then she might as well be dead.

With each step Alexandra's pace increased. So did the tension inside her. Every muscle in her body was bowstring tight. When the light changed and the flow of traffic brought her to a halt, she felt like a river suddenly dammed.

As she bounced up and down with nervous angry energy she noticed a brown bottle lying in the gutter. Her mouth watered. The stress was getting to her—and a very familiar feeling was taking over. *I need a drink,* she thought, remembering the blessed escape that only alcohol could bring.

She gritted her teeth. Would she never quit having these cravings? Wasn't it enough that she'd nearly destroyed her future once? She knew alcohol wasn't the answer. "It's a crutch," she muttered to herself. "It's a temporary fix. You'd only feel miserable tomorrow. . . ."

But I feel pretty miserable right now.

The light changed and she dashed across the

street, shame burning her cheeks. Just yesterday at the hot line she'd told Rodin that cravings were nothing to be ashamed of. It wasn't quite so easy to convince herself right now. Advice was a lot easier to give than to take.

Or was it?

Was she only kidding herself to think that she'd helped Rodin? What if he'd listened politely and then gone right on feeling ashamed and inadequate? Or worse—what if he'd just put down the phone and picked up the bottle? What if he'd complimented her just because he was grateful that she'd taken the time to talk to him?

No, Alexandra told herself, stopping her runaway train of self-doubt. *I'm good at the hot line. Rodin sounded totally sincere when he said I'd helped him. So I should believe it.*

Just thinking of that sweet-voiced caller seemed to calm her. Her pace slowed, and she began to relax a little.

Maybe Rodin is the kind of guy I need for a boyfriend, she thought. *We would help each other through tough times like these, not cut each other down. I bet he wouldn't create problems by preaching at me.*

Alexandra sighed, trying to picture what Rodin looked like. She figured he was tall, with broad shoulders and chiseled cheekbones. He probably wore a lot of black to match his longish hair and mysterious, sexy dark eyes. But his eyes could be soft too—just like his voice. He'd sounded so patient and understanding on the phone, even though *he* had called *her* for help. Since he'd chosen the pseudonym of a famous sculptor, he was probably an artist—someone who'd respect her creative side, not attack her for it like *one* guy she knew.

She wiped tears from her eyes. It just wasn't fair. There she was, just beginning to learn she had a talent for art, and all Noah did was make fun of her. Rodin would never—

This is crazy, she told herself. What was the use in fantasizing about a person she'd never even meet?

Still, she was glad that she'd been able to help him yesterday even if she never spoke to him again. Working at the hot line had been a lifesaver for Alexandra from the start. It had proved that old saying that the best way to help yourself is by helping others. Nothing failed to take her mind off her own problems and stave off the alcohol cravings like a feeling of being needed.

So why am I heading to the dorm, where I'll only sit and pout and feel sorry for myself? she asked herself. *Why go back to my room and try to fight the cravings alone? Work. That's what I need!*

Alexandra turned around and headed toward the hot line office.

*　　*　　*　　　　　　　　　　•

Am I in the right place? Alexandra thought as she entered the hot line's outer office. Gone were the tacky but welcoming fake flowers, the tattered ecology posters, the never-empty Mickey Mouse candy dispenser. Also missing was the vast pile of junk mail that had always buried the front desk. They had all been replaced by one new, surprising element.

Sitting behind that bare desk was a thin, serious-looking stranger. From his red buzz-cut hair and his ramrod-straight posture, she wondered if maybe he hadn't wandered over from ROTC by mistake. He even seemed to be in uniform, with his very *un*stylish dark knit pants and button-down long-sleeved shirt.

"Hi. Where's Doug?" she asked, referring to the grad student who'd been in charge of the hot line ever since she'd started working there.

"Doug doesn't work here anymore," the guy said with a sneer. "His ecology grant came in, so he's off to Yellowstone to study grizzly bears or something equally ridiculous."

"Oh," Alexandra said weakly, unable to come up with an appropriate comment. Besides being slightly taken aback by the new guy's tone, she was also somewhat disappointed. She really liked Doug Chandler. He'd trained her at the hot line and shown her how she could really make a difference with her volunteer work. "So . . . who are you?"

"Fred Hoffman," the guy said, jumping to his feet. He wasn't extremely tall, but because of the rigid way he stood, he seemed to tower over her. Looking up, she could see the reddish stubble on his chin that she supposed was the beginnings of a goatee. "I've been assigned to run the hot line from now on. And you are?"

"Alexandra Rollins."

His gaze scanned down her body as if she were on display. "What can I do for you, Alexandra Rollins?"

"I work here."

"Hmmm." He sank back into the desk chair and began to shuffle through a stack of file folders. "I don't remember seeing your file anywhere. Rollins, you said? Are you new?"

"No. I've worked here for several months now."

Cindy Lee, who had evidently been manning the phones, appeared in the doorway behind Fred's back. She rolled her eyes, pointed to Fred, stuck out her tongue, and mimed gagging.

Alexandra lifted her eyebrows, amused, but tried to keep her face passive.

"I thought I had all the files here," he grumbled. "But I don't seem to have an Alexandra Rollins." He turned and checked the schedule on the bulletin board above his desk. "You're not on the schedule either," he said in a tone that seemed to imply that their little conversation was now over.

"I know it's not my day to work," she explained. "I just came by to see if you needed any help."

Fred's silence made Alexandra feel awkward and somehow stupid. She searched for a way to make her purpose more clear. "Doug was always having trouble finding volunteers for the middle of the day, so he got stuck manning the phones a lot of times. Sometimes I'd drop by and let him take off for a late lunch."

"No reason for that. As you can see, Cindy's here."

"But not for long," Cindy quipped. "Great timing, Alexandra. I just happen to be due for a lunch break."

Fred turned a scowl in Cindy's direction, but she grabbed her purse and was out the door before he could stop her.

"This is inexcusable," he complained. "I can't have people coming and going whenever they please. If that's how Doug ran things, then it's no wonder this place is such a mess." He searched through the file folders once again. Finding the one he wanted, he scribbled something furiously with a thick black marker. "From now on we'll be sticking strictly to schedule," he announced grandly. "Lunches will be taken at desks, not out of the office."

Alexandra cleared her throat timidly.

Fred looked up at her as if he were surprised she was still standing there. "Well . . ." He tossed the marker into the top desk drawer. "OK. I guess we *can* use you for a while, then, Alexandra. Because *I* don't plan to cover for every little irresponsible volunteer. I can't stand slackers. I expect every single one of my volunteers to pull their own weight. Got that?"

Alexandra fought back a crazy urge to salute. "Got it."

"And don't think that just because you're filling in for an hour or so now that it will excuse you from your regularly scheduled times. I have big plans for this place. Eventually I hope to have the hot line open twenty-four hours a day—with at least one operator on duty at all times. But it's going to mean extra hours for everyone."

"I don't think we have enough—"

He yanked at the cuffs of his shirt. "Do you have a problem with extra hours? If you do, then maybe you aren't the kind of person we need working here at the Substance Abuse Hot Line. We need dedicated workers—hard workers—people with a well-developed sense of responsibility."

Alexandra closed her eyes and sighed. *Do this.*

Don't do that. Responsibility! This guy sounds just like Noah—except worse.

"Next week's schedule is posted over the phones. You might want to check it while you're here. I expect everyone to show up exactly when scheduled. No excuses. I don't go in for any of this trading off and expecting someone else to cover your butt. Because if everyone expects *me* to come to their rescue, then they're going to be sadly mistaken. I'm a senior. I have way too much to do to be at everyone's beck and call."

He took the phone from the top of his desk and dropped it into his bottom desk drawer along with his stack of file folders. Then he pulled out a large ring of keys and proceeded to lock every one of his desk drawers, starting at the bottom and working his way up. When he was finished, he looked again at Alexandra. "Any questions?"

"Nope. I think you've covered about everything."

"I believe I have." He leaned forward with both hands flat on top of the desk. "Well, now that you're here, I'm going upstairs to the psych lab. There are a couple of research articles I need to copy. Think you can handle the place alone for about an hour?"

Alexandra bristled. "I think I can manage."

She stood frozen in front of his desk until she heard the door shut behind him. Then she spun around, clicked her heels together, and brought her right arm up in an exaggerated salute. "I think I can manage very well, *sir!*"

What a jerk! she thought as she slipped her book bag off and shoved it under her chair. She checked the newly posted schedule and saw that her hours had indeed been doubled. "Thanks a lot, Mr. Fred Hot-air-man." She jotted the times on a sheet of scrap paper and tucked it into her pocket.

Her stomach growled loudly. "And thanks to you too, Noah, for making me miss lunch!" She walked over to the low table where the hot line's coffeepot normally sat, only to find a handwritten sign propped against the sugar bowl. Use Coffee Vending Machine Upstairs.

"Unbelievable!" she groaned. "What a condescending, superior, pompous . . . egotistical . . ." Frustrated that she'd run out of negative adjectives, Alexandra snatched up the sign and tried to rip it in half. But the cardboard was thick, and she only managed to bend it. Tossing it to the floor, she plopped into her chair and began to dig through her book bag. Surely she had something—a piece of candy, a stick of gum. "The nerve of that guy, coming in here thinking he could boss everyone around . . . change everything . . ."

Alexandra suddenly realized that she was even

more worked up than she'd been on her way to the dorm. That wasn't what she'd come to the hot line for—not at all. She'd wanted to forget her problems, not create new ones. "I'm here to help others," she reminded herself. "I'm here to help. . . ."

She laid her head on her hands. *Maybe I'm overreacting,* she mused. *Maybe Fred's not that bad a guy. I was still feeling angry at Noah, that's all. Fred's probably just a little nervous about starting here. He was trying to be firm, and my disappointment about Doug leaving made him feel inadequate or something.*

Alexandra was still trying to convince herself when the phone rang. "Hello, SVU Substance Abuse Hot Line," she answered as pleasantly as she could manage.

There was no reply, but she could hear someone breathing on the line. She waited patiently. It wasn't unusual for people to panic when she answered. Sometimes it took people a while to work up enough nerve to reveal their problems.

As she expected, the silence was followed by a long, deep sigh. "I'm here to listen," Alexandra coaxed. "How can I help you today?"

"Oh, baby," a deep voice rumbled. "I thought you'd never ask."

Alexandra blinked in surprise. This was *not* the shy reply she'd been expecting. But maybe she was reading the voice wrong. Some people with substance abuse problems also had communication problems, she knew. Maybe she'd misinterpreted the caller's tone. It was easy to do when you couldn't see his face.

"Do you have a problem you'd like to talk about?"

"Not unless you want to talk about those tight jeans you're wearing."

Alexandra gasped and instinctively looked down at her legs. But then she rolled her eyes at her silly reaction. Sure, she *was* wearing jeans, and admittedly they were a little on the tight side. Still, there was no way this guy could know what she was wearing. He had taken a lucky guess. And why not? At any given time, over half the girls on campus had on jeans.

"They're really hot. Is that why they call this a *hot* line?"

Fraternity prank, she thought disgustedly. It wasn't the first time. One time a caller pretended to die of an overdose while Alexandra was trying to help him. When she screamed and burst into tears, the guy started laughing and making fun of her. It had taken her weeks to get over that prank. She couldn't believe there were bozos out there who thought it was fun to belittle something as important as the hot line. The mere idea infuriated her.

"I'll admit you look really cute in that Theta

sweatshirt," the caller continued, "but it hides your figure. How about wearing a sexy dress tomorrow? Something with a really short skirt. . . ."

Alexandra tensed back up. Jeans she could explain away, but how did this guy know she was wearing a Theta sweatshirt? There was no way he could see her. The back room of the hot line office had a couple of windows, but the shutters were always down. The front office didn't have any except for one long, narrow pane of reinforced glass in the door. Evidently it was someone who knew her—someone who'd decided to play a prank on her after seeing her go into the hot line office.

Her emotions bounced between nervous and angry. She chose angry. "Is there anything else you wanted to talk about besides my choice of apparel?"

"No. You talk. Talk to me with that sexy, toe-curling voice. Do you know what your voice does to me? It sends chills from my spine to . . . well, you can imagine where it sends me. Want me to describe what's happening to me this very minute?"

"No!"

"Oh, but I think you do. I think you'd love to hear it as much as I'd love to tell you. And you're really going to love it when I describe what's going to happen when we finally meet."

Alexandra slammed down the receiver. Fraternity prank or not, the guy had gone way too far. *Great,* she thought. *The perfect ending to a perfectly rotten day.* Even the hot line had let her down.

Doug had warned her, back during her training, that she'd get calls from crazies. It couldn't be helped. Any business dependent on phones was subject to idiots who got their laughs from making obscene calls to women. "Just hang up," he'd told her. "Don't give them an audience. That's what they want. It's usually harmless."

"*Usually* harmless," Alexandra muttered. "Just a nutcase playing a prank." But all the same, the call left a very bad taste in her mouth. All she could hope was that the guy wouldn't bother calling again.

Chapter Four

I must be crazy, giving in like this again, Noah thought as he tapped on Alexandra's door early Tuesday morning. _But let's face it. I can't stand life without Alexandra._

After their little fight in the cafeteria, he'd hoped Alexandra would call him and apologize. Every minute that he hadn't been at work or in class, he'd spent beside the phone waiting for her to call—but she hadn't. Once again it was up to him to make the first move toward making up.

He frowned and knocked again—more loudly this time. The door opened.

"Hey, Noah," Trina said groggily. "What's up?" She pushed her long dark hair out of her face and grinned at him. Leaning there against the door in pink fuzzy pajamas with feet, she looked like an escapee from the campus nursery school.

He smiled. "Hey, Trina. Sorry I woke you, but I was looking for Alexandra."

"You just missed her. She left for the cafeteria about fifteen minutes ago. Want me to give her a message when she gets back?"

"No. That's OK. Maybe I'll try to catch up with her at the cafeteria. I was just hoping we could have a little time together."

"That's a good idea. I know she'd be glad to see you. She was as grumpy as an old witch when she came in last night. And she looked really down this morning. I thought something was bothering her, but she didn't say what. Maybe she'll talk to you."

Noah took off so quickly, he didn't even hear whether Trina shut the door. All he cared about was catching up to Alexandra. If she seemed depressed when she left her room, then maybe—just maybe—that meant she was missing him as much as he was missing her. He ran all the way to the cafeteria.

Alexandra was easy to spot. She was sitting at a table by the window—alone. The sunlight practically glimmered in her hair.

"Alex!" he called. She looked up and waved. *That's a good sign*, he assured himself. *At least she didn't shake her fist or throw a biscuit at me*.

Suddenly he was hungrier than he'd been in days. "Everything," he said to the cafeteria server without paying much attention to what was being dished onto his plate.

He took his loaded tray, added a cup of coffee and a huge glass of milk, and hurried over to Alexandra's table. "I stopped by your room and Trina said you'd be here."

"And here I am," she said. She pointed to his tray with her fork. "What's with the jock breakfast? Getting ready to go into hibernation?"

He grinned sheepishly. "I didn't eat much yesterday. I'm starved." He pulled out the chair opposite her. "It is OK if I sit here, right?"

"Sure. There's no law against it. None that I know of anyway." There was just a hint of annoyance in her words—just enough to let him know that she hadn't forgotten their argument.

"OK. I guess I deserved that." He sat down and began unloading his tray. "I know I've been sort of short-tempered lately."

She shrugged and dabbed a chunk of pancake into a puddle of syrup.

"Alex, I'm sorry about yesterday," he said. "I nearly called you the minute I got back to my room, but—"

"It's just as well you didn't," she interrupted. "I wasn't there. I spent most of the afternoon working at the hot line."

Noah looked down at his plate. He really did have a lot of food there—eggs, bacon, toast, hash browns. To fill in the awkward silence, he picked up a piece of the toast and started spreading apple jelly on it. But the toast was dry and hard. It broke and crumbled onto the plate, leaving jelly on his fingers.

Without a word Alexandra scooted the napkin dispenser over in front of him.

"Thanks," he said. He yanked out a napkin and wiped his fingers.

Alexandra busied herself cutting the rest of her pancakes.

"Alex, I came over here to try and work this out, but if you don't want to talk—"

"It's not that I don't want to talk, Noah. But I have sculpture class in a few minutes. A *responsible* person like *me* wouldn't want to be late—even if it is just a hobby class!" She laid her knife on the edge of her plate with a forceful clank.

"Well, I'll try to be brief." Noah could practically feel the acid pumping into his stomach. He cleared his throat and tried to calm himself. "I know I lost my temper yesterday, and I'm sorry, but I don't know what's happening between us anymore. I feel like you're ignoring me. It hurts me that—"

"I'm not ignoring you, Noah."

"You are, and you don't even see it. I'm worried about you. You're changing and . . ."

"And what?"

"And it's not a change I particularly care for."

"Well, pardon me!"

"Don't get all defensive. I'm trying to tell you what I think the problem is."

Alexandra rolled her eyes. "I can hardly wait."

"Well, it's like this thing you have about denying Enid. Last semester in Abnormal Psych we were studying dissociative disorder—you know, where a part of a person's personality gets separated from the rest—"

"Noah, did you come over here this morning to tell me you think I'm insane?"

"No!" He took a sip of coffee and winced when it burned his lips. "I'm just trying to say that I'm worried about you."

"Well, just because you got an A in Abnormal Psych doesn't quite mean you're ready to psychoanalyze me or diagnose me or whatever it is you think you're doing. I don't have a split personality."

"I'm not saying you *have* a dissociative disorder, Alexandra. I'm just saying that it seems like you're having a hard time zeroing in on who you really are."

"*I* know who I am. *You're* the one who doesn't seem to know who I am!"

"College can be a time of stress and anxiety."

"You're the only thing causing me stress at the moment."

Noah winced. "I know you'd like to believe that, but sometimes when people are under stress, they don't want to admit where it's coming from. They lay the blame on something else entirely and—"

"What psychology text did you get *that* from?" Alexandra picked up her glass of milk and drained the last swallow. "Never mind," she said, wiping off her milk mustache. "I don't really care." She wiped her hands and threw her napkins on her tray. "How can you sit there and say I don't know about stress? This is Alexandra Rollins you're talking to. Don't you remember coaxing me out of the bottle about a thousand times? Or have you forgotten T Squared?"

"I thought *you'd* forgotten."

"I'm beginning to wish I could!"

Noah shook his head. "That's your answer to this whole problem, isn't it? You think you can just cut me out of your past the same way you cut out Enid. Just go on with your life and pretend I never existed." Noah ran his hands over his face, exasperated. "You can't just chop off your past like it's bad hair, Alex. It's there. It'll always be a part of you, whether you like it or not."

"Well, that's where we disagree—strongly," Alexandra said defiantly. "You *can* chop it off— bad hair, bad past, or bad whatever. A person is perfectly free to walk away from it if it's not what they want. I'm living proof. Back in high school I was powerless to change because everybody knew me as Enid. They wouldn't let me change. But going away to college gave me my chance for a new life, so I grabbed it. Nobody knew me, so I could become the person I always wanted to be."

"And *this* is who you always wanted to be?"

"Yes, *Alexandra* is exactly who I wanted to be. Who do you *think* I should be?"

"I'll tell you what I *think*. I think I'm tired of talking to Alexandra. You'd do well to adopt a few of Enid's old traits. It wouldn't hurt you to care—"

"What's the deal with you and Enid lately? When we first met, you didn't even know Enid ever existed."

"Well . . . I look at you sometimes and wonder, what was Enid like? Was she really so different?" He cleared his throat and ran his hand nervously through his blond hair. The gaze his girlfriend was leveling at him was positively poisonous. "I mean, I think you're a smart, sensitive girl—"

"Woman."

"*Woman* who's trying to hide behind a mask. Look at you, Alex. How much time did you spend putting on your makeup this morning?"

Alexandra's green eyes widened. "What kind of question is that, Noah? What do you care?"

"I'm just saying, Enid was the kind of girl who didn't care about those things. They're really not that important."

"You don't know Enid," she snapped. "You never knew her. She doesn't exist anymore."

"And your skirt, Alex," Noah continued shakily. "Don't you think it's a little too short?"

Alexandra gasped and pushed away from the table. "What . . . what are you getting at, Noah?" she asked quietly. She no longer looked angry—just terrified somehow.

"You don't need to dress up like some kind of . . . I don't know . . . sorority party girl," he finished as diplomatically as he could. "That's not the Alexandra I know. You're not cheap or shallow, but sometimes . . . sometimes you make yourself look that way."

"I can't believe I'm hearing this." She started gathering up her things. "You have no right—*no right* to talk to me that way, Noah. This"—she gestured toward herself—"this is Alexandra Rollins. This is who I am. So don't start playing with my mind like this. Don't start bringing up my past, OK? *Alexandra* is who you fell in love with, not Enid."

"Alex." He reached across the table and caught her arm. "You *are* Enid Alexandra Rollins—not two people. The girl I love is Enid . . . Alexandra . . . Rollins."

"Stop talking to me like I have amnesia or something." She jerked her arm free. "I'm not the one with a problem. You are. I took Psych 101 too, Noah. I think your sudden need for me to regress is due to *your* lack of identity. Maybe

64

you'd better dust off your old textbook and study up on your own insecurities. Try the chapter about obsessions and paranoia!"

As she scrambled to her feet Noah reached out for her hand again, but she dodged him.

"I've got to get to sculpture class. Excuse me," she said coldly. She picked up her tray and stormed off.

What's going on? Noah wondered, tears burning behind his brown eyes. *Why can't we even talk anymore without ending up in a huge argument? Maybe Alexandra is right. Maybe I am insecure.* No longer in the mood to eat, he pushed away his food.

Is it me? he asked himself. *Am I afraid that if she keeps changing, she'll leave me behind? That there won't be room in her life for me if . . .* Noah shuddered. He didn't even like to imagine life without Enid Alexandra Rollins. The truth was, he never, *ever* wanted to let her go.

Running late for sculpture class—thanks to Noah—Alexandra dashed into the studio and slipped into the first empty chair just as the lights were going out.

Terry Mackinaw, SVU's thin, balding, flamboyant assistant professor of sculpture, noticed. "Glad you could join us, Alexandra," he said cattily. Terry frequently thought he was being funny when he was simply being a pain.

"Happy to be here, Terry," she shot right back at him. She was too angry at Noah to put up with any bunk from Terry "I-just-want-to-be-your-buddy" Mackinaw.

He pursed his lips in a mild show of disapproval and continued with the introduction to his lecture. "Today we are going to be discussing two very important aspects of three-dimensional art—movement and texture. Through the use of slides we will examine the work of master sculptors in an attempt to understand how they used these two techniques to create *reality*." Terry stressed the last word dramatically. But then Terry did everything dramatically. While he was *dramatically* messing with the slide projector, Alexandra opened her book bag and pulled out her notebook and pen.

When she got settled, she noticed that the guy next to her was watching her. Luke, that guy who had offered to clean up her pottery mess when she was in such a hurry to go meet Noah for lunch—not that her rushing did a bit of good. Noah hadn't appreciated it at all.

Luke quickly looked away. He seemed to be blushing, but it was hard to tell in the darkness of the studio.

Terry finally mastered the projector, and the first slide appeared on the wide pull-down screen at the front of the room. Alexandra flipped open her notebook and got ready to take notes.

"In Ernst Barlach's piece *The Avenger*, movement is implied by the figure's forward thrust and the long, sweeping horizontal lines of the robe. What else do we find in this statue that conveys movement?"

"What about that big sword the dude has over his shoulder?" someone in the back of the room suggested.

"What about it?" Terry asked. "Can you be a little more specific?"

The student couldn't.

Bending low over her notebook, Alexandra used the long, painful lull that followed to try and write down the name of the statue, its artist, and Terry's comments about movement. She was just about to get it all down when an arm shot up next to her.

"What about the way the figure's head is projected forward away from the shoulders?" Luke's voice was soft, pleasant . . . familiar somehow. *Of course it's familiar,* she thought. *I just talked to him yesterday.*

"Very good point," Terry replied. As Terry began to explain more about the use of movement Alexandra jotted down a few notes and sneaked another peek at Luke out of the corner of her eye.

He was actually a lot cuter than she'd first thought. Yesterday if someone had asked her to pick Luke out of a lineup, she'd have been hard-pressed to do it. She'd have described him as tall-ish, medium build, medium brown hair cut in an ordinary way—but she hadn't really been paying much attention then. She'd been too worried about what Noah's reaction would be to her being late.

Now that she was looking more closely, she could see that Luke was actually quite hand-some—even sexy in a quiet, gentle, tender way. His brown hair was the exact color of a teddy bear she used to have—and probably as soft. The light from the screen reflected off his eyes, making it hard to read what color they were.

He caught her staring, and it was her turn to be embarrassed. Still, she didn't look away. She couldn't if she'd tried. She was stunned, frozen by Luke's eyes. They were incredible—hazel, she supposed, because they weren't really brown, not really green or blue, just sort of a medium change-able color with a tinge of sadness to them. The kind of eyes that made her melt. The kind of look that stopped her heart.

She blinked and forced her attention back to Terry, hoping Luke didn't think she was crazy. Two or three more slides were discussed in terms of movement, and then Terry began talking about texture. Alexandra smiled, amused by the way he seemed to get so involved with his subject.

". . . so you see, texture is extremely important in sculpture. The very texture of a face can reveal a great deal about a person."

Alexandra glanced back at Luke's face. *Now there's texture,* she thought. His cheeks were smooth, with a sort of perpetual blush to them. She wondered if they'd feel as soft and satiny as they looked.

Luke caught her looking again . . . and smiled.

Alexandra stifled a sigh. If she hadn't thought he was handsome before, his smile would have done the trick. It was gorgeous. He had perfectly straight teeth and dimples that seemed to set off his wide smile in parentheses. Alexandra felt her face grow warm.

Luke nodded toward the professor, reminding her that she should be paying more attention.

"For example," Terry continued, "compare these two magnificent pieces. Auguste Rodin's *Danaïde* and Donna Forma's *Soul's Replenishment.* Very similar, yet created almost one hundred years apart. Notice how in each the smooth figure of a woman seems to be rising from the rough surface of the stone. The incredible contrast between the harsh, rough rock and flawless polished marble makes the skin seem young, lustrous. Unbelievably lifelike." Terry clasped his hands in front of him as if he were a little child saying a bedtime prayer. "How could one even look at either of these sculptures without wanting to reach out and touch it!"

A new slide flashed onto the screen and Terry pointed. "On the other hand, on this craggy face notice how the worn, lumpy quality emphasizes the subject's age and probably traumatic history. Can anyone identify the title of this sculpture?"

"The work is *Little Man with the Broken Nose*," Luke replied.

Alexandra couldn't help but be impressed by Luke's knowledge of art. Same for Terry—he was positively beaming at Luke. "That's correct. And who is the sculptor?"

"Rodin," Luke answered.

An electric current shot through Alexandra. She knew that voice. She blinked up at him, and he nodded an embarrassed confirmation. He was the caller from the hot line—Rodin!

"And what about Rodin's work impresses you the most, Luke? You seem to be quite familiar with the artist."

The brilliant blush stayed on Luke's cheeks, but he answered calmly. "I think I'm most impressed with the fact that he overcame his past to achieve great art."

"Maybe it's the other way around. Maybe his art was great because of his past," someone in the back of the room argued.

Suddenly the class was launched into a discussion

of how a person's past affects his or her artistic pro-
ductivity. But Alexandra didn't participate. She was
too busy watching Luke.

Overcoming the past, she repeated in her mind.
*Luke understands all about that, I bet. Luke would
probably understand me better than Noah does. Maybe
I should just give up on crabby old Noah and . . .*

Alexandra began to gnaw at a fingernail. The
crazy thoughts that were running through her
brain made her feel guilty and disloyal. Noah was
a good boyfriend despite his little tantrums. And
they were totally committed to each other. She
really loved him . . . didn't she?

After Terry had packed up his slides and left,
Luke looked over at Alexandra, who was putting
her notebook into her bag. The fact that she'd
recognized his voice had embarrassed him slightly,
but he trusted her. He wasn't afraid she'd reveal
his secret to anyone else.

"I'm staying to work on my project," he said
boldly. "How about you?"

Alexandra sighed. "I wonder if I should
bother. Maybe the world has enough lopsided
bowls. What are you working on anyway?"

"A self-portrait bust in clay. It's one of the re-
quirements for admission into the fine arts program.
Evidently the art department here at SVU is big
on self-portraits. Every class I have—oil painting,

watercolor, photography—they've all assigned self-portraits. I guess they want to make sure I'm able to re-create myself in any medium."

Alexandra seemed to drift off for a moment. She stood up quietly and looked down at her hands for such a long time, Luke began to feel he'd done something wrong. "I'm sorry. Did I say something—"

"No. I was just thinking."

"Alexandra," he said gently. "I know you recognized my voice—"

"It's OK, Luke. Really. I mean, you recognized mine too, right? Your secret is safe with me. Everyone who works for the hot line is sworn to the strictest confidentiality."

"I know. I was just going to say, I'm glad you know it's me. Now maybe I can just talk to *you* about it sometime. You know, in class or somewhere besides the hot line."

"Sure, Luke. Anytime."

She seemed to drift away again. Leaving her to her thoughts, Luke went to the back shelf and took down his project.

When he returned, she was still standing in the same spot, staring out the window. "You seem really preoccupied today, Alexandra."

"Most everyone calls me Alex."

"If you don't mind, I like Alexandra. It sounds more . . . more like you."

"Thanks, Luke. Believe it or not, that means a lot to me." She smiled sadly.

He uncovered his statue, put on his glasses, and began manipulating the clay. "Do you want to tell me what's wrong?"

"Nothing's wrong. I'm fine."

"Something's bothering you. I can tell. You look like your mind is a million miles away."

"No, not that far."

"Come on. You can tell me. I'm Rodin, remember? What's the worst I could do, make a sculpture out of your problems?" He began to scrape away clay with a wire loop to create cheekbones. He rolled the excess clay into a long coil and began adding pieces to the ears.

"Why are you making the ears so big?"

He blushed. "It's supposed to be a self-portrait. I'm not trying to prettify myself."

"But your ears aren't that big."

"Tell my mother that. She calls me her little Dumbo. All my life I've been teased about my ears."

Alexandra smiled. "I think you have very well proportioned ears."

At the moment he felt as if his big ears were on fire. How he wished he could control his stupid blushing! He scraped a little clay off the top of each ear and stepped back. "How's that?"

"Better, I think."

"Well, now that you've learned another of my

deep, dark secrets, it's about time you leveled with me. What's causing those little frown wrinkles on your forehead?"

She sighed. "It's my boyfriend. He's been giving me a hard time lately. He's getting so jealous of the time I spend away from him. I'm beginning to think that he wants me to be at his beck and call every minute of the day."

Luke scowled. "He sounds like a selfish guy . . . although I can see where he'd want to keep you all to himself." He froze for a second, afraid he'd gone too far.

"No. He's not selfish. Not usually," Alexandra said defensively. "He's just worried about me. That's all. He seems to think I'm changing."

"Everybody changes. That's life."

"That's what I told him. But Noah doesn't agree. He thinks I should be exactly the way I was back in high school."

"Back when you two first met?" Luke asked. He looked at her over the top of his glasses.

"No. That's the funny thing. He didn't even know me in high school—and I wasn't anything like I am now. I was this shy little nobody." Alexandra dragged a stool up beside him and leaned her elbow on the worktable. "I don't tell a lot of people this, but I didn't even use the same name." She leaned toward Luke and lowered her voice. "Would you believe my first name is actually

Enid? Isn't that the world's most drab name? It's no wonder I was a nobody."

"I can't believe you were ever a nobody." Luke took a deep breath and readied himself to take the plunge. "You're too pretty and too—"

"Believe me, I wasn't pretty then," she replied. "I was *dull*. But I don't ever want to go back to being that pathetic little creature. I sometimes have nightmares about returning to high school and being trapped in Enid's world forever."

Luke stopped working. He couldn't help gazing into her beautiful green eyes as she talked.

"Don't you think people should grow?" she asked. "Just because someone is stuck being one way in high school, that's no reason to keep being that person forever, is it?"

"Of course not. It's like I was saying earlier in the class discussion. People have to be able to overcome their pasts."

"The way I see it," Alexandra explained, "it's like . . . well, what if you were going somewhere, and after a long way you realize you're on the wrong road. There's nothing wrong with leaving that road and looking for another one, is there?"

Is she talking about her own problems or mine? he wondered, amazed. He'd never known anyone so perceptive and honest—especially not so soon after first meeting. But he knew Alexandra's words were real—they reflected his own feelings exactly

75

about change and the past. She'd even known how he felt about needing a drink when he was down and lonely. There was more depth to her than he'd even dreamed.

"But listen to me," she said with a laugh. "I'm rambling on and on—I'm not even letting you get your work done. Besides, I don't have to convince you, do I? If you didn't believe a person could change, you would never have called the hot line."

Luke blinked. He didn't want her to leave. He never wanted this conversation to end. He felt as if he could talk to her for years. "About the hot line," he began quickly. "I want you to know that you really were a big help. I got the impression that you understood my problem completely."

"As long as we're sharing secrets, I might as well tell you one more. There was a time when I turned to alcohol too. That's how I knew what you were feeling when you said you really craved a drink." She reached up and wiped away a dab of clay from his cheek as if it were the most natural gesture in the world.

Luke felt dizzy from her touch. He knew that Alexandra shared his view on a lot of things. And she *was* staring at him during the lecture—quite a bit, actually. Was there a chance in the world that she could feel for him the same way he felt for her?

Chapter Five

No more, Trina Slezniak thought. She slammed her history book shut and laid her head on top of it. She'd been trying to study ever since lunch, but she couldn't concentrate with all the sighs and moans coming from Alexandra's side of the room.

"OK, Alex." Trina threw down her pen. "What's making you so miserable? When Noah showed up to get you for breakfast this morning, I thought you two had made up."

"I thought we had too, for about three minutes. But then all he did was criticize me."

"That doesn't sound like Noah. Usually he can't say enough good things about you."

"Usually he'll listen to reason too, but not lately." Alexandra spun her chair around so that she and Trina were facing each other. "I don't know what's gotten into him. He's not acting like himself at all. I know he's tired and upset, but that doesn't make his crabbiness any easier to put up with. He hadn't been at my table five minutes when we got into another huge argument. It was Saturday night all over again."

"You mean the Enid mess?" Trina asked with a sigh. Saturday night, after she'd returned to their dorm room and asked about the shredded photo on the floor, Alexandra had given her a blow-by-blow account of her fight with Noah. At first she thought Alexandra was overreacting. Trina really liked her roommate, but it was no secret that Alexandra had always been overly touchy about her past. She figured that Alexandra had blown this whole Enid mess way out of proportion. But if she and Noah were still arguing about it, maybe there was more to it than she'd first thought.

Trina turned off her desk lamp and gave Alexandra her full attention. "Want to tell me about it?"

"There's nothing to tell. It's the same old thing we fought about Saturday night and yesterday too."

"Did you bring up Enid or did he?"

"He did . . . I'm sure." But her expression didn't look very certain. "I'm sure it was Noah. Why on earth would I bring her up! I'm the one who wants to forget her." She sighed loudly. "Sorry, Trina. I know I'm being a pain. But I don't know what to do."

"I don't know either, Alex. It just sounds so uncharacteristic. I really like Noah. He's a nice guy, and he adores you."

"Well, next time you see him, would you do me a favor and remind him?" she asked with a laugh. "It seems he's forgotten."

Trina opened the minirefrigerator she kept beside her desk and pulled out a can of soda. She held up a bottle of mineral water to Alexandra. She nodded, and Trina tossed it to her. "Alex, don't get mad at me for saying this, but I'm getting the feeling that maybe there's something else going on. I can't believe all this moaning and groaning is just because Noah wants you to accept your past."

Alexandra took a long swig of the water. "What are you getting at?"

"Well . . . is there a new guy in your life?"

"What are you doing, trying out for the Psychic Roommates Network?"

"Yes." Trina pressed her fingers against her temples, closed her eyes, and began to sway. "Now I'm getting a vision from beyond. . . . I sense that you are avoiding my question. . . . But wait. There's more. I see a new guy . . . someone hot."

Alexandra sputtered and nearly choked on the mineral water. "Wow! That's incredible!"

"Oooh, do tell." Trina opened her eyes, pulled her legs up onto her chair, and waited anxiously for the scoop.

"Hot guy, huh?" Alexandra scoffed. "I think you must be getting vibes about the hot *line*. There's a new guy there."

"Is he really hot?"

"Hotheaded, maybe. His name is Fred Hoffman. And I think he must be Hitler's great-grandson. He's a senior, but he thinks he's the boss of the world." Alexandra mock pulled at her hair. "I swear, you give some people a little power and wham, it goes right to their head. When I walked in there to work yesterday, he treated me like some rank beginner. At least when Doug was there he made me feel like I was a capable human being. But this guy . . . sheesh!"

"Alex—"

"And thanks to Fred Hitler-Hoffman I'm working again tonight. He's actually doubled everyone's hours. Can you believe that?"

"Uh-huh. I believe you about this Hoffman being a slave driver, but I'm not buying him as the cause of all that moaning and groaning and deep thinking you've been doing over there."

"OK, Madame Slezniak, keep looking into your crystal ball. Maybe you'll find something . . . like a Mind Your Own Business sign."

Trina laughed. "C'mon, Alex, give. What are you hiding? I've known you from the first day of school, remember? I heard the tales about Mark Gathers. I recognize the faraway looks and—"

"Well, maybe you are psychic. But I guess that's better than being called psycho. That's what Noah thinks I am."

"Back to the subject, roomie. Is there a new guy in your life or not?"

Alexandra flopped across her bed and pulled a pillow to her chest. "Well, there isn't another guy—yet. But I've been sort of wondering if there could be."

Trina quirked an eyebrow. "Hmmm, interesting. Do you mean you're tired of Noah and you're out shopping for a new guy or you've seen someone that you're interested in?"

"Well, there's this guy in my sculpture class."

"Now we're getting somewhere." Trina moved over to Alexandra's bed and sat down beside her. "Has he asked you out?"

"No. He's really, really shy, but we've spoken a few times. He's sort of cute in a quiet, artsy way. The sensitive type, you know."

"I thought Noah was the sensitive type."

"He is. I mean, he used to be, but I'm not sure anymore."

"Alexandra, are you certain this is the right thing to do? You and Noah are so good together. I'd hate to see you throw it all away over some fling."

Alexandra laughed sadly. "I'm not so sure I have much choice. Noah practically told me to go find myself a new boyfriend."

"He did not!"

"He did. He suggested I get a fraternity guy. Someone more to my liking."

"Is this art guy in a fraternity?"

"I wouldn't think so. But he's cute. You'd like him, Trina."

From where Trina sat she could see two framed pictures on Alexandra's desk. One was of Noah, the other of Noah and Alexandra together. The two of them looked so happy. They'd made it through a lot. Trina hated to see it all go down the drain.

"I think you should be careful here, Alex," Trina began. "Noah doesn't deserve to get dumped. This new guy might be fun, or he might not be. But why throw away a perfectly great relationship just because someone catches your eye when you and Noah are having problems? Noah might be a little confused at the moment, but he's still a great guy."

Alexandra followed the line of Trina's gaze and picked up Noah's picture. "You're right, Trina. Noah deserves better. What we have is definitely worth fighting for. I'll just have to make him understand how I feel."

"You're late," Fred snarled the moment Alexandra arrived at the hot line for her newly extended hours.

"I'm supposed to be here at five," she countered. "And it's five right on the dot." She double-checked her watch and held it out for Fred to see.

"You're supposed to be *working* at five. Most people are bright enough to realize that means arriving five or ten minutes early to get settled in."

"Well, it doesn't take me five or ten minutes to settle in, Fred." She plopped down in her chair. "See? I'm settled."

Normally she wasn't so snippy and sarcastic, but something about Fred's superior manner instantly brought out the worst in her. She had been right about him after all—he *was* a world-class jerk.

"Another thing," he said, snatching up his ever-present stack of file folders. "No personal calls." He began pecking on the folders with the eraser end of a pencil. "You should know that, Alex. These lines are for students with substance abuse problems only."

"Fred, lighten up. How could I have been making personal calls? I just got here, remember? Anyway, the three phones back here only take incoming calls. If I wanted to dial out, I'd have to use the phone on your desk in the outer office."

"I know that!" he barked. "And you can bet it'll be locked up whenever I'm not around. But that's not what I'm talking about. Some chick named Jessica has called here twice this afternoon looking for you. This is not your sorority answering service, you know."

Just what I need. Someone else nagging me about the sorority, she thought, sighing much louder than necessary. "Sorry, Fred. I'll try to make it clear to Jessica that she's not to call me here."

"I believe I've already set her straight on that account."

Alexandra lifted her hand in front of her mouth to cover her grin. The very thought of someone like Fred thinking he'd set Jessica Wakefield straight on anything was laughable. *Better men than you have tried and failed in that quest, Sergeant Hoffman,* she said silently.

She scooted closer to her phone, hoping he'd take the hint and go away. But he stood there practically at attention, looking down his nose at her. "And as long as we're setting people straight," he continued, "we have another little problem we need to discuss."

Alexandra groaned. "What other problem do *we* have?"

"It's your tone."

"Sir, yes, sir," she barked. "I'll try to be more respectful, sir!"

"Very funny," he snarled. "A little more respect on your part would be refreshing, but I was referring to your phone tone."

"*Phone* tone?" Alexandra looked up, hoping to see a spark of redeeming humor in her new boss. The steely glint in his blue eyes told her he was dead serious.

"As I said, this isn't the sorority house. Don't try to be so cheery on the phone. The students who call the hot line have heavy problems. Answer in a serious voice. Exude confidence. Let these people know immediately from your tone that you mean business and can help them. The way you answer, you sound like a telemarketer—or a flirt."

Alexandra seethed. She absolutely did *not* need this! For the past few months the hot line had been her sanctuary. It was a special place where not only could she help others, but she was helping herself. Now Fred was making her sorry she ever volunteered.

"Be serious. Businesslike—"

"Got it, Fred," she said, cutting him off to take a call.

While some poor guy talked about his roommate's drug problem, Alexandra spoke in as serious and businesslike a tone as she could manage. Finally Fred took his file folders back to the outer office. Alone at last, she turned her face toward the wall so her voice wouldn't carry. Returning to her normal voice, she finished up the call the best way she knew how—with friendly sympathy and understanding. The caller

85

seemed to cheer up almost instantly, and he responded to Alexandra's suggestions with the kind of seriousness and concern that told her she was making an impact on the guy's life—and hopefully his roommate's too.

When she hung up, she looked over her shoulder and jumped. There stood Fred and his file folders again.

"One more thing," he said.

"What?" Alexandra practically screamed in frustration.

"Why did you lie to me?"

Alexandra slumped down in her chair, confused beyond belief. "I have no idea what you're talking about, Fred. And I'm really not in the mood for any more of your criticism—however constructive you might think it is. How about saving some for tomorrow?"

"You didn't lie?"

"No!"

"Then you're not Enid Rollins?"

Alexandra's mouth dropped open. What in the world was going on? Were Noah and Fred forming the Enid Rollins fan club or something?

Fred pounced forward. "Just as I suspected!" He cradled his precious tan cardboard folders and pulled one from the stack. "I was afraid I'd either lost a file or you were an imposter, but now this makes perfect sense." He leaned on the edge of her cubicle. "What are you trying to hide?"

"Nuh-thing."

"Then why did you tell me your name is Alexandra Rollins?"

"Because it *is*."

"Well, it says here, and also on your official school registration, that your name is Enid."

Alexandra counted to ten and let out a slow, calming breath. "My first name *is* Enid. I don't use it anymore. I go by my middle name, which is Alexandra."

"You changed your name? Really?" He tucked the folders under his arm and moved in so close, Alexandra got a crick in her neck just looking up at him. "How junior high! I'm surprised you didn't change it to Barbie or Skipper."

Alexandra bit back the urge to tell him exactly what she thought of the name Fred. "Listen, Fred, what I call myself has nothing to do with how I do my job."

"It might. Besides being completely immature, name changing is frequently a sign of an unstable mind. A fragmenting of personalities. It usually indicates that one is dealing with someone unsure of their identity."

Jeez! What is it with these people? Alexandra pressed her palms over her ears and scrunched up a handful of hair on each side of her head. "I suppose you're a psych major too."

"As a matter of fact, I am."

She let go of her head and stared into his stern face. "Well, I wish you *psycho* majors would wait until you get your Ph.D.'s before you start analyzing victims!" she screamed. "Some people don't appreciate it!"

"*Evidently* some people *need* it."

"*Evidently* some people need to learn to mind their own business."

He tapped the file folder with his stubby finger. "It also says here that you have a drinking problem."

"I don't care what it says," Alexandra said angrily. She didn't feel she had to explain herself to this overbearing creep. "Who gave you the right to snoop through that stuff anyway? All you need to know is that I show up on time, I do my job, and I'm reliable."

"Correct on all counts. And the point is, you don't sound very reliable to me."

Alexandra resisted the urge to strangle him. "That's absurd. Name one unreliable thing I've done since I've worked here."

"I can't, but that doesn't mean I'm not concerned." Fred blinked rapidly, and Alexandra noticed his red lashes were practically invisible. "I'd rather prevent problems before they happen than have to deal with the consequences later. Life is much cleaner that way. And I have serious doubts as to whether you can help other people when you so obviously need help yourself. What we don't need here is the blind leading the blind."

"OK, I give up." Alexandra made a show of gathering up her things. She was beyond tired of this conversation and of Fred in general. "So am I fired or not?"

"No. You're not fired. But I just want you to know that I'm keeping a very close eye on you. The first minute I think you aren't pulling your weight, you're out of here."

Alexandra turned her back to him. For several minutes he continued to breathe down her neck—literally—and she recoiled in disgust. At last she heard him march back to his desk and methodically lock up all his drawers. "I'm heading back to my dorm for a sec. Don't you dare go anywhere." The front door slammed. Then silence.

"Fred McHitler has left the building," she announced grandly. But clowning around didn't cheer her up any. She laid her head on her hands and tried to keep from crying. It seemed as if her whole world was falling apart—or more realistically that everyone *in* the world had caught some kind of Enid virus. She'd thought her old self was successfully buried, but suddenly everyone wanted her to turn back into the dishrag of Sweet Valley High.

"Yep, I'll bet good old Fred would love having

Enid bowing and scraping around here, blindly obeying him like a little frumpy puppet," she mused, her sense of humor quickly vanishing into a dark, deep pit of anxiety. A tear fell from her eye and dropped with a damp plop onto Fred's freshly photocopied work schedule.

"What's happening to me?" she asked herself as sobs overtook her. "Why is Enid Rollins *haunting* me?"

He chuckled as he listened to the sound of the phone ringing at the other end of the line. "I know you're there," he sang. "Come on, baby. Answer the phone. I want to hear your voice."

"SVU Substance Abuse Hot Line."

A shiver skittered up his spine as her voice came across the line. Fierce and uncontrollable, like electrical stimulation. He held his hand against his chest in an attempt to calm his wildly beating heart. Something about her sexy voice drove him crazy.

"SVU Substance Abuse Hot Line," she repeated. "This is operator number three."

Man, she sounded cool. So cold, butter wouldn't melt in that luscious mouth of hers. But he could tell that it was all an act. He grasped the phone more tightly, ready to give her what she needed. Suddenly he wanted to torment her. Scare her. Break her free from that icy shell. Let her be who she really was deep inside. *Force* her to be—

"Is anyone there? How can I help you?"

A hint of strain, not good. She'd hang up soon, he knew. He'd let her suffer long enough. "Help me?" he began, his voice aching. "Ohhh . . . I can think of a lot of ways."

He heard her sharp intake of breath. Then the line fell silent. But he could tell she hadn't hung up. He licked his dry lips. "How's this for a change?" he asked. "I'm calling to help *you*. And I *can* help you. You do believe me, don't you?"

"H-How can you help me?" she asked nervously.

"I can help you understand. I know you 'cause you're just like me. You're torn in two." He waited and smiled. The very fact that she had stayed on the line told him he was right. "Tell me your name."

"We don't use names here at the hot line."

"Come *on*. You can't hide from me. I know exactly who you are, and I want to—"

The line went dead. He stared at the receiver a moment in disbelief. Then he threw it across the room. With a single stroke he swiped everything from the surface of his desk. Still his body continued to pump adrenaline. He picked up a chair and threw it. He kicked his bed.

"I can't stand your scorn!" he yelled at the dead phone. "You're meant to be mine always. I must possess you. You can't ignore me. *You can't ignore me!*"

He yanked open his bottom desk drawer and pulled out a large hunting knife. "I have to make her see," he murmured. "I have to make her see that she's meant for me." He squeezed the wooden handle of the knife. It fit his hand perfectly. He held the knife up to the window, admiring the way its sharp blade glinted in the sunlight.

She'll realize how much she needs me soon enough, he thought. *She just needs a little help, that's all.*

Slowly he ran his finger across the edge—just hard enough to feel the sharpness of the smooth steel but not hard enough to cut himself.

"I think it's time for some carving."

Chapter Six

"Hey, Alexandra!"

The moment Alexandra stepped through the front doors of Theta house on Wednesday morning, she looked up to see Lila Fowler motioning to her from in front of the elaborately decorated reception table.

"Alex," Lila called again. "Just the girl I wanted to see! You're an artsy person. Give me your honest advice. Don't you think those camellias are just *too much* in that flower arrangement?"

Alexandra stepped back and examined the bouquet thoughtfully. "Well, they *are* the official Theta flower . . . but I guess they are pretty big." Alexandra knew her answer was vague, but she also knew that it didn't matter. Lila was going to do whatever Lila wanted to do.

"That's exactly what I thought," Lila said,

pulling three or four big white camellias out of the arrangement. "Oh . . . Denise was looking for you. She was afraid you were going to be late."

Alexandra sighed. "It seems like 'late' is my middle name these days. But this time it wasn't my fault. I got ready in plenty of time, but then I couldn't find my dorm keys."

"Oooh, I hate it when that happens," Lila said. She rearranged the remaining flowers to hide the gaps and turned back to Alexandra. "Where'd you finally find them?"

"I didn't. I looked everywhere. I dumped everything out of my book bag and went through my purse about five times. I even checked the pockets of the jacket I wore yesterday. I've got my car keys, but the dorm keys? Nope."

"That's too bad, but they'll probably turn up. I lost the keys to Bruce's Porsche once—and would you believe we found them in the refrigerator?"

"I sure *hope* they turn up," Alexandra said. "The housing office charges a fortune to make a new lock. And not only that, they take forever."

"Why don't you just have some dupes made?" Lila asked.

"I can't—not until Trina comes back. She left this morning to go visit her parents. She won't be back till Sunday."

"*Quel* drag."

"I know. So I didn't even bother to call the housing office. I just left my room unlocked. Trina will probably throw a fit when she comes back, but . . ." Alexandra shrugged. "I couldn't very well miss this big-sister reception, could I?"

"Well, you're looking good," Lila said with a grin. "That's what matters most. I love the effect of that boxy jacket over the tight dress. And that russet color on you—perfect. It makes your hair really stand out."

Alexandra stood a little straighter and ran her hand down the side of her linen tank dress. For Lila to compliment her outfit was the ultimate high. Lila spent a good deal of her incredible wealth on designer clothes. No one in the sorority had better fashion sense than she did.

"Did I hear you say someone's hair was sticking out?" Jessica asked. She snuck a crab canapé out from under the covered silver tray.

"No. I said Alexandra's new outfit makes her hair stand out—as in shine, glow. . . . Say, you're wearing that lavender cashmere sweater again, Jess," Lila teased. "That's two times this week. Can we say fashion faux pas?"

Jessica rolled her eyes. "Can we say give me a break, please?"

"Can we say lay off the hors d'oeuvres?" Lila smacked Jessica's hand as she went in for another steal.

"Who died and put you in charge of the refreshment table?" Jessica complained.

"Magda did—well, she didn't *die,* but she did saddle me with the refreshments for this soiree."

"That's what you get for bragging that you were friends with that hot new caterer—Mr. Party-frog-wah, or whatever his name is." She licked cream cheese off her finger and turned to Alexandra. "I was supposed to tell you that Denise is saving you a seat. She's over there at the blue couch by the windows."

With an indulgent grin Alexandra left Jessica and Lila to argue about caterers and frogs and whatever other tangent Jessica could send them on.

She breathed a sigh of relief as she collapsed onto the pale blue velvet couch. It felt good to be in a place where she could laugh and be lighthearted for a change. With all the turmoil that had been going on in her life lately, she'd almost forgotten how to have fun.

"It's about time you got here," Denise Waters said. "I saw your name on the big-sis roster. Are you excited?"

"Sort of. I've never gotten to be a big sister before."

"Me neither. Did you remember your pin?"

Alexandra patted her pocket. "I've got it right here."

With a toss of her glossy jet-black curls Isabella

Ricci joined them on the couch. "You girls ready for your big-sister assignments?" she asked excitedly. "I sure hope I get someone decent this time."

"They are all decent, Izzy. They couldn't be pledging Theta if they weren't," Denise reminded her.

"Oh yeah?" Isabella raised a perfectly arched eyebrow and cocked her head toward the door, where Alison Quinn stood surveying the room with her nose in the air. "You were saying?"

"OK," Denise admitted. "A few snooty ones slip past every now and then."

Alison considered herself to be the queen of the sorority instead of merely the vice president—or vice pain-in-the-butt, as Alexandra preferred to call her. Alison had a few loyal subjects, but Jessica, Denise, Isabella, Lila, and Alexandra would never be counted among them.

Alison tinkled a little brass bell, signaling that it was time for the ceremony to begin. As conversations broke apart and girls scattered toward chairs, Lila pushed her way between Isabella and Denise and commandeered enough space for herself and Jessica, who had stopped in front of the ornate antique mirror to check her lipstick.

As they all shifted to make room Alexandra was left practically hugging the arm of the couch, but she didn't mind. In fact, she would have gladly crammed in another body or two. She loved being with her sorority sisters. It was the one place in the world where her identity was not being questioned. Every woman on that couch thought of her only as Alexandra—and they accepted her just the way she was. They never picked apart everything she did, never psychoanalyzed. They never dredged up her past and told her who she ought to be.

The only ones in the sorority who even knew that she used to be Enid were Jessica and Lila. Jessica seemed to have forgotten—and more than likely, Lila never gave it a thought one way or the other since it really didn't have anything to do with her.

"Ahem! Attention, everyone," Alison brayed. "Since our president, Magda Helperin, just *couldn't* get away from her Western Civ exam this morning"—she rolled her eyes—"it is my duty and privilege to now call this meeting to order."

Jessica looked over at Alexandra and gagged. Alexandra nodded and pinched her chin between two fingers. Jessica giggled at Alexandra's reference to Alison's pointy chin. Alexandra propped her elbow against the arm of the couch, leaned against it, and smiled. It felt great to be on the inside of a joke for a change. The very fact that Jessica accepted her was concrete proof that Enid no longer existed.

And Noah thought he was insulting me when he accused me of turning into Jessica, she thought with a smile. She could think of worse things to be, that was for sure. *Wake up, Noah,* she told him mentally. *Who* wouldn't *want to be Jessica Wakefield?* Jessica's name was practically a synonym for fun. She always had a party to go to and a major hunk to take her there. Even back when Alexandra disliked Jessica, she still envied her lifestyle. Jessica had it all: boyfriends, beauty, excitement, popularity, and a sense of fun.

Alison's nasal voice temporarily bored its way into her brain. ". . . and it's of the utmost importance that we get each of our pledges off to a good start. That's the ultimate goal of the big-sister tradition. Because no one knows the importance of being a Theta like a Theta. . . ."

Alexandra thought about that. It *was* important being a Theta. Especially to her. Sometimes she felt that if she hadn't pledged Theta, she'd have slipped back into being Enid a long time ago. Theta Alpha Theta wasn't just her doorway to popularity—it gave her a sense of camaraderie and support as well. For the first time in her life she had lots of good female friends. In a way, it was the glue that held her self-confidence together.

"Remember, pledges," Alison droned on in her obviously memorized speech. "Your big sister is the person you're to go to if you have questions about Theta Alpha Theta or even about your schoolwork in general. If they don't have the answers, they will direct you to someone who does.

Your big sister is more than your mentor. She should be your best friend." She smiled ingratiatingly and lifted her hand. "So with that in mind, I will now assign each Theta pledge her big sister."

After a smattering of applause Alison started down her list. Alexandra waited anxiously. It seemed to take forever for Alison to get to her.

"Susan Zercher," Alison announced grandly. "Come receive your pledge pin from your big sister, Alexandra Rollins."

Alexandra stood up, and a pretty young blonde bounced toward her. "I was hoping I'd get you," the girl whispered exuberantly.

Alexandra smiled and opened the envelope containing the gold-and-ruby pledge pin she'd brought with her to the ceremony. Carefully she pinned it to Susan's blouse. "Sisters forever," Alex said—the Theta motto.

"Sisters forever," Susan repeated. She and Alexandra shook hands.

Alison stepped back into the center of the room and nodded to Kimberly Schyler, indicating that it was time for the closing ritual. Kimberly didn't even pretend that the speech was her own. She pulled out a three-by-five card and read: "Pledges, the gold in these pins symbolizes purity of thought and deed. The ruby stands for the fire and passion for life and learning that burns inside each Theta. Never forget, this pin is more than a symbol. It is a way of life. Through Theta you must strive to become a well-balanced person who is unselfish in her service to others and, above all else, loyal to her sisters." Finished, she folded the card and sat down in her chair with an unceremonious plop.

"Remember, pledges," Alison added, smoothing down her overly sprayed hair. "Your pin must be worn at all times. Any pledge caught without it will be subject to dismissal. Wear it on the left over your heart—exactly where your big sister pinned it. No other pin or jewelry is to be worn above it. Cherish this pin. Someday you will pass it on, just as you will pass on the traditions and values of Theta Alpha Theta."

With the official part of the meeting over, conversations resumed, girls began to drift toward the refreshments, and the pledges and actives moved together to get better acquainted.

Susan scooped up Alexandra's hand and squeezed it. Her blue eyes sparkled with her bubbly personality. "Alex, I meant what I said earlier. I really *was* hoping I'd get you for my big sister. I've read all about you in the actives booklet. It said that in addition to your sorority duties, you volunteer at the SVU Substance Abuse Hot Line."

Alexandra glowed. "Yes. It takes a lot of my time, but I think it's important."

"Oh, I agree. I think it's so great that you'd

give up your free time to help other people."

I wish Noah could hear you say that, she thought.

Susan sighed. "Sometimes I think I'd like to do something like that, but I don't know if I ever could. I really respect your courage and devotion."

Alexandra couldn't get over the way Susan stared at her with such open admiration. *She doesn't think there's anything wrong with me,* Alexandra thought. *Is that the way I look when I'm talking to Lila and Jessica? Does Susan wish she could be me, the way I sometimes wish I could be them?* It was an oddly exciting thought.

The moon was covered with clouds, and the cool breeze hinted of coming rain Wednesday evening as Noah and Alexandra walked silently across the quad. Noah shoved his hand deep into the pocket of his jacket. It was pretty clear that Alexandra had no desire to hold it. She seemed to have a circle of invisible insulation around her that he hadn't been able to penetrate all evening.

Noah had hoped that by taking Alexandra to Pasquale's, her favorite Italian restaurant, her mood would improve. It hadn't. Dinner had been a disaster. Their conversation—what little there was of it—had been painful and stilted. Both of them had obviously tried to avoid any mention of difficult topics, but that didn't leave much to talk about these days. No matter what he said, Alexandra always seemed to take it the wrong way. Noah felt as if he'd been having dinner with a total stranger.

Now the walk back to the dorm was just as awkward . . . no, it was worse. At least at Pasquale's they'd had forks and glasses to occupy their hands and comments on the food to bridge the strained silences. Here they only had each other. Now instead of forced polite conversation, they were reduced to saying nothing at all.

Noah was so wrapped up in replaying the disastrous date in his mind that he was startled when Alexandra tugged at his arm.

"Let's sit over here awhile," she said, nodding toward one of the concrete benches in the grassy quad. "I think we need to talk."

Noah's heart took a nosedive. There was a certain hollow hopelessness in her tone that alarmed him. But he followed Alexandra to the bench and sat down. He could feel the cold concrete through his jeans, but it wasn't nearly as cold as the lump in the pit of his stomach. His whole body felt frozen inside.

"Noah, I know that things haven't been going very well between us lately. I don't know what's wrong—not completely. But one thing I do know. I need for you to respect me."

"I do. You just—"

She placed a finger over his lips. "Please, let's not start arguing again. Just let me say this. The thing is, *I* don't feel like you respect me. Maybe it's my problem. If so, I'll have to deal with it, but if I can't level with you about how I feel, then I guess we don't have as strong a relationship as I thought we had."

Noah shifted on the cold concrete and tried to take Alexandra's hand, but she edged away and crossed her arms protectively across her chest.

"I get the impression lately that you don't see me as who I am," she said. Her words sounded almost rehearsed. "You see me as who you want me to be. But what about who I want to be? That's important too, isn't it?"

"Of course it is, but—"

"You're holding me back, just like Elizabeth used to do. I know you don't mean to be so . . . smothering, but I feel like you won't let me grow."

Noah's world went out of focus. *Had she said grow or go?* he wondered. Did it even matter? He knew where this whole talk was leading. Just as he feared, he was getting the brush-off. She wanted him out of her life so she could devote all her time to being a sorority girl. She wanted to flit among the top echelons of campus social life and leave Noah Pearson far behind. *She wants to dump me!*

Noah gnawed at his bottom lip and tried to

push aside his insecurities, but it was impossible. He'd never cared for anybody the way he loved Alexandra. The thought that she might be outgrowing him or tiring of him had been eating away at his insides for weeks. Now it had consumed him completely. He could think of nothing else. *And life without Alexandra . . .*

He propped his elbows against his knees and buried his head in his hands.

"Noah! Are you listening to me?"

Swallowing hard, he looked up and tried to focus on her words. They sounded blurred, like his vision, which was clouding with tears.

"I mean this, Noah. I love you, but I want you to let me—"

"Go?" he yelled. "Is that what you want?"

"Noah," she gasped. "Please. Don't be this way."

He jumped off the bench and began to pace in front of her. "No, I can't. I can't let you do this. It's not . . . it's not that easy. I can't just let you go! Not without a fight."

"A *fight*? Noah, don't talk like that!"

Noah couldn't believe he had let his temper go out of control again. He wanted to punch himself for yelling at her like he did. He'd been trying all night to keep his cool. But now his anger spilled out like blood. He was more furious than he'd felt in years.

105

How could Alexandra do this to him? He'd been the one to help her get over that stupid jock Mark Gathers. He was the one who'd helped her stop drinking and get her life and her schoolwork back on track, and this was how she repaid him. To just dump him without another thought. *Good old Noah—he's a great transitional boyfriend, but not someone you want to spend the rest of your life with. Thanks for helping out, but now I don't need you anymore. Click.*

Noah dropped to his knees in front of her and pried her hand loose from its invisible armor. "You talk about respect—well, I could use a little of that too," he said, willing his voice to be calm. "I thought we were in love. Have I meant no more to you than . . . than . . ." Words failed him, but he had to strike out with something. He couldn't just squat here on the grass, looking like a fool. He dropped her hand and climbed to his feet.

"Where would you be without me, I wonder?" he snarled. "What about how I helped you deal with your drinking problem? You certainly needed your doormat Noah then, didn't you?" He clamped his mouth shut and stepped back. Why did he keep lashing out when all he wanted was for her to love him . . . for things to go back to the way they were before? It was as if there was another side of him that was fighting to get out. . . .

Alexandra stood up defiantly. "Don't you dare yell at me, Noah Pearson! I'm sick of it! I am not some little pet project that you can write a psych paper on. I am a real person."

"Are you?" Noah pressed a finger against her Theta pin. "You used to be, but are you still?"

She angrily shoved away his hand. "That's the stupidest thing I've ever heard."

Noah clenched his fists and closed his eyes. It took every ounce of self-control he could muster to keep himself from exploding. Only with the most supreme effort was he finally able to get ahold of himself.

"Sorry," he apologized impatiently. He rubbed his throat and tried to bring his voice back down to a more civil level. "You're right. That was a stupid thing for me to say."

"Yes, it was," she agreed, but there was no hint of forgiveness in her voice.

"Maybe we need some time apart to cool off," he suggested with his last ounce of control.

"Maybe we do," she agreed—much too quickly.

A swirl of sadness engulfed him. He'd hoped she'd protest. If she'd just ask him to stay, he would . . . forever. It was everything he wanted in the world.

But Alexandra tilted up her head and stood her ground, not coming a fraction of an inch closer. Her eyes glittered in the lamplight. All Noah wanted to do was scoop her up in his arms and press his lips against hers. But her invisible barrier seemed to be growing. "Alex—"

"How long of a cooling-off period do you need, Noah? A night? A month? Forever?" She gazed up at him, her green eyes detached and far away, as if it really didn't matter one way or the other.

If only he could wrap her in his arms, attempt to recapture what they'd lost—but neither of them moved. "I guess we'll just have to see how long it takes," he muttered under his breath. "But before this is over, I'll make you see how much you need me. Just watch."

Before he could allow her to see the tears that were welling in his eyes, he turned and stalked off, leaving her standing under the lamppost. Alone.

Alexandra kicked a rock and sent it skittering down the sidewalk. "Take all the time you need!" she shouted as she watched Noah's back disappear from sight. As mad as Noah was right now, it might take aeons for him to cool down. She'd never seen him so furious. She hadn't even known he was capable of such anger. It had actually frightened her. "You can cool off till you freeze, for all I care!"

With a sigh she dropped back down on the bench. Alexandra was more confused than she'd been in ages. She felt as if she were stuck in some bizarre science fiction movie where everything was the opposite of what it was supposed to be. Noah had always been the most patient person she knew. It was one of the things she loved most about him. But where had all that rage suddenly come from? Could Noah be losing it?

Maybe I don't really know him as well as I thought I did. He seems so preoccupied with knowing who I am. All his ranting and raving about how I've changed and how he doesn't know me—it's just a bunch of . . . excuses. He's the one who's changing. But who's he turning into? Or should I say what!

She looked up into the dark sky, almost hoping to see a full moon. But that only explained monsters in movies and books. Besides, there was hardly a sliver of moon showing, and it was mostly covered with clouds. She shivered and shoved her hands into her pockets.

Noah's anger didn't make sense. All his excuses, all his attacks . . . Was he just covering up his own problems? Maybe so, but she knew one thing. She'd seen a side of him tonight that she definitely didn't like. A side she never knew he had. A side that terrified her.

Chapter Seven

"Answer, my love. Answer the phone," he urged. Holding the receiver to his ear with his shoulder, he leaned against the phone booth and jabbed the point of his knife into the side of it. Slowly and deliberately he began carving a heart around a very large capital *E*.

Finally her precious voice came over the line.

"SVU Substance Abuse Hot Line."

"Hello, my love," he said.

"Oh no," she groaned.

But her reaction didn't anger him. No, he was flattered and happy that she had recognized his voice. It meant he was making progress. "Wait, don't hang up . . . *Enid!*"

Hearing her gasp into the phone, he let out a long, satisfied breath. He knew that would get her attention.

"Who is this?" she whispered hoarsely.

"Your own true love."

"Where did you hear that name?"

"I have my sources."

"What sources?"

"That's not important." He paused from his carving and took the phone more securely in his hand. "The important thing is that we are meant to be together. I know it, and you know it too. Admit it."

"I'm hanging up."

"No! Don't hang up on me! Admit it. I want to hear you say out loud that you're meant for me." He leaned his forehead against the *E*. "You'd know it's true if you'd take a good long look at yourself. Say it. . . . Say it now, Enid. Say you were meant to be with me." He could feel the power surging through his veins. His hands were starting to tremble.

"Listen, you. I don't even know who you are—and I don't want to know. I want you to leave me alone."

"Enid, don't hang up on me. I'm warning you." He listened to her shallow, frightened breathing on the other end of the line. He loved the way it sounded—like the beating of humming-bird wings. Beautiful. "Terrible things will happen if you hang up on me again."

"I'm calling the police."

"That would be the biggest mistake of your life. And maybe the last."

She said nothing, but he could imagine her eyes wide with terror and her breath warm and rapid against the phone. The idea sent pulses of ecstasy through his body. He closed his eyes and lowered his voice. "I thought this was supposed to be a help line."

"It is, but I can't help you," she said.

"Maybe not, but I can help you. And even though you aren't being very nice to me—yet—I fully intend to. That's just the kind of guy I am. I know about you, Enid. I know *all* about you. You are good and true. It's only when you're with your friends that you change."

A sharp intake of breath, then—silence.

"I know who your true friends are," he continued, "and I know who only *pretends* to be your friend. There are certain people who are leading you astray, and we can't have that. Some of your so-called friends wouldn't think I was good enough for you. I can get rid of these people for you, Enid. I can do anything to help you achieve your destiny."

"I don't want your help. Just leave me alone!"

He winced as the line went dead. He stared at the buzzing receiver in disbelief for a moment, then replaced it.

How could she hang up on him again? Hadn't he warned her?

Slowly and deliberately he gouged out the last inch of the heart on the phone booth outside the Theta Alpha Theta sorority house. Then with a puff of breath he cleared the fiberglass particles off his knife and slipped it beneath his jacket. Zipping the jacket just enough to hold the knife in place, he turned and marched up the wooden steps of the Victorian sorority house. Although the floor squeaked slightly, the TV was blaring. So no one noticed as he opened the door to the lounge and stepped inside.

It's a prank, Alexandra told herself again. *It's just a bad, warped, prank phone call.* But that argument was no longer having any effect on her nerves. She couldn't even pretend to believe it anymore.

This was no obscene caller who picked names at random from the phone book. This wacko was someone who thought he knew her—someone who had targeted her especially for this abuse. And he was getting worse. Now he was threatening her. He'd warned that terrible things would happen if she hung up on him. What kind of terrible things? She didn't really want to know.

But she *had* hung up on him. Now what? Was something going to happen to her? Was he going to be waiting outside when she left the hot line? Would he follow her to her dorm? To class? Would he try to hurt her? Was it her *last* mistake?

Maybe I shouldn't have hung up on him, she thought guiltily, *but I just couldn't take that deep, raspy voice another second*. Just the thought of it sent fresh shivers up her spine. *And the things he said!*

If she understood his ramblings correctly, then he had also threatened her friends. What had he meant by erasing bad influences? He'd said he'd get rid of people who led her astray. Did he mean that he'd frighten them away from her, or . . . did he mean "get rid of" in the gangster movie sense?

Alexandra covered her face with her hands. "I'm going crazy," she muttered through her fingers. Fear was just making her paranoid. Of course this guy wasn't really going to hurt anyone . . . was he?

Alexandra got up from her chair and began to pace around the tiny office. "He can't be serious!" she told herself.

But he sounded serious. He sounded so sure of himself—so crazy.

After a couple of laps around the room she plopped back down in her chair and hugged herself. She looked longingly at the empty table where the coffeepot used to be. She could sure use a cup of good, strong hot coffee right now. Maybe something even stronger. Her hands felt like ice, and she was starting to shiver.

"I've got to tell someone about this guy," she said, jumping up from her chair. But almost instantly she closed her eyes and sank back down. "I *can't* tell anyone." She was blocked by another hurdle—the hot line's rule of confidentiality. Was she prepared to throw away her credibility and possibly even the hot line's just because some crazy caller's threats scared her silly? If she blabbed something a caller told her, how could any caller ever trust her again?

In her mind she could see Doug Chandler's kind face. He was telling her that all information heard over the Substance Abuse Hot Line had to be kept totally confidential. "Nothing said in this room goes outside these walls," he'd said.

She wanted to argue with Doug. She wanted to scream, "But this case is different!" But it was essentially an argument with herself—an argument she knew she was going to lose. Because deep down, Alexandra truly believed the policy of keeping every call private was right. She knew that firsthand.

Alexandra thought back to the first time she'd called the hot line. If she hadn't been assured right up front that her calls were secret, she would never have been able to tell a soul about her drinking problem. She laid her head in her hands and moaned. She owed the hot line so much, her unquestioning loyalty seemed a small price to pay.

Who knew where she'd be right now if she hadn't trusted the hot line? In some bar, probably. Or dead in some drunk-driving accident. The kind of accident that took the lives of others too . . .

She shook her head wildly, desperate to clear away her ugly thoughts. But Alexandra couldn't let it rest. This wasn't exactly a regular call. As the caller had said, he wasn't asking for help. But if he was even slightly serious about the things he said, he definitely *needed* help—more help than anyone Alexandra had ever come across!

Maybe he was just some harmless kook letting off steam by calling the hot line instead of someone on campus. But maybe he was a psychopath who really intended to carry out the threats he was making.

I can't keep this to myself, she realized. *I really believe he's dangerous. He could hurt me—or somebody else—without thinking twice. He said so himself!*

Alexandra glanced at the clock. She still had another hour before Cindy was supposed to start her shift. But by then it might be too late. Besides, she couldn't take being cooped up in the office anymore. The walls were actually starting to close in on her. She felt she'd go crazy if she sat here listening to her own thoughts for another second.

She didn't even bother to flick on the recorded message. She just grabbed her purse and headed out onto the quad and toward campus security as fast as she could go. Fred would be furious when he found out she'd left the phones unmanned, but he'd have to get over it. This was an emergency. Lives were at stake!

Halfway to the campus security office her doubts returned. She slowed her pace almost to a crawl. *If I march in there and tell* them *this, they're going to think* I'm *the one who's crazy*, she realized. *What am I going to say, "Someone called and said he loves me"? "I think he's going to hurt someone if I don't love him back"?*

No, this wasn't a problem for campus security. She just needed to talk to someone. Sort out her own fears and feelings. What she needed was a friend to talk to, but who could she trust? She'd always been able to talk to Noah, but with the way things stood between them right now, she'd probably have better luck with strangers at the security office.

The only close confidant she'd ever had was Elizabeth Wakefield, her best friend from high school. But they rarely spoke anymore. Anyway, Elizabeth was Enid's friend, not Alexandra's. Elizabeth had never really accepted the change. And Alexandra certainly didn't need another person reminding her about Enid. And now that she thought about it, Elizabeth would probably only lecture her. She definitely didn't need another

117

lecture. Fred and Noah pretty well had that base covered.

Suddenly she became annoyed. *I'm scared, so what am I doing?* she asked herself. *I'm thinking like Enid! I'm looking for Enid's friends to escape to—not Alexandra's friends. Alexandra has friends—lots of friends. A whole house full of friends!*

Alexandra did an about-face so suddenly that the guy bicycling behind her nearly had a wreck. She sputtered an apology and as quickly as she could, she hurried toward the Theta Alpha Theta sorority house, all the way across campus.

He lifted the knife high into the air and brought it down with double-handed force. Again . . . again . . . and again he stabbed Jessica Wakefield. Then stepping back, he smiled and admired his handiwork. The deep red pattern widened against her soft lavender sweater like a blooming flower.

He took a deep breath and stepped even farther back so he could take in the whole scene. It was perfect. Symbolic. Cinematic. There in the prim and proper Theta Alpha Theta TV room, Jessica's shapely body lay slumped forward against the coffee table, with all that blond hair falling over her face in a curtain that almost brushed the floor.

He'd done it. He had stilled her superior, sneering, sorority girl attitude forever.

His momentary calm subsided, and rage began to bubble in him again. Just the very thought of Jessica enraged him. Perfect blond sorority girl! Leading his Enid astray with her snobby put-downs and haughty laughter. She was bad news. Bad, bad news. Totally wrong to be Enid's friend. But now thanks to him, she was no longer a temptation for his precious little wren. His Enid was safe from Jessica's contamination.

Suddenly Jessica's arm slid from the couch cushion. The sudden movement sent him into another spasm of hate. He leaned over the back of the couch and stabbed down again savagely—again . . . and again. The arm didn't move. It dangled limply between the couch and the coffee table.

With a final yank he pulled the bloody knife away and wiped it on the back of the couch. "I wonder if Enid will want to be like you now," he murmured.

Without looking at her face, he reached around the dead girl and tore her sorority pin from her sweater. He shoved it into his pocket, but it wasn't enough. He needed more proof. Jessica and all these sorority girls put so much emphasis on clothes and jewelry. It was part of their problem.

No telling how much Jessica had spent on those fancy earrings. Well, they'd do nicely. He'd save them for someone who deserved such elegant beauty. As if he were plucking ticks off a dog, he yanked the earrings from her ears.

With one last look around, he pulled off his jacket just in case it had any telltale blood spatters, rolled it into a ball around the knife, and tucked the bundle under his arm. With a deep, calming breath he slipped out of the sorority house as quietly as he'd entered.

He was still on the walkway when he heard horrified screams coming from the TV lounge. Ducking his head to hide his broad smile, he strolled away nonchalantly, blending in perfectly with the steady stream of students walking to classes.

Arms swinging and head tucked down, Alexandra hurried along Fraternity Row. That wasn't the real name of the area, of course, but that's what it was called by SVU students; all the fraternity and sorority houses lined both sides of the street for several blocks. Theta house was just off Fraternity Row, on Cherry Street. Alexandra was only a few steps from where Cherry Street veered to the left when she heard someone call her name.

She looked up and cursed her bad luck. Fred "Boom-Boom" Hoffman, in the flesh.

He clamped a heavy hand on her shoulder. "Where are you off to in such a hurry?" he asked.

Alexandra wriggled free. "Theta house." *If it's any of your business,* she added mentally.

"Well, whoop-de-do. How nice for you." He leaned down and peered into her eyes. "I thought you were supposed to be on duty at the hot line until five," he said accusingly.

"I am . . . or I was, but . . . well, something came up."

"Not finishing your shift. That's not very professional or *responsible,* is it? Weren't we just speaking about that Tuesday?" He readjusted the package he was carrying under one arm and ran his hand over his bristly chin. "I have to warn you, Alex. This isn't going to look very good on your record."

As Alexandra opened her mouth to tell him just what he could do with her record, a police car squealed past. It swerved around the corner wildly, its lights flashing and siren blaring.

"What the—," Fred blurted. As he turned to watch the car Alexandra could finally see around his puffed-up frame. She raised her eyebrows in surprise. Right down on Cherry Street an ambulance and two police cars were already parked. The third car screeched to a halt with its front tires right on the lawn of—

"Oh, look." Fred cocked his head to the side.

"Something big must be going down at—"

"Theta house!" Alexandra screamed. Her heart lurched. She shoved past Fred and sprinted toward the scene. Her sorority sisters were gathering out front. Everyone looked like they were . . . crying? It was hard to tell. Whatever it was, it was serious.

Alexandra dashed up the steps to the porch, where Denise was consoling one of the new pledges, Caryn Stokes.

"What's happened?" Alexandra asked.

"She's dead," Denise whispered, continuing to pat Caryn's back. Tears streamed down her face. "Caryn found her—"

"Who?" Alexandra cried.

Isabella and Lila wandered by, holding each other. "Oh . . . my . . . gosh," Isabella sobbed. "I can't believe it. I just can't believe it."

"What?"

"Stabbed, like, a hundred times." Lila moaned as if in shock, her brown eyes bloodshot. "Right in the TV lounge. In the middle of the day. She's gone. I can't believe she's gone."

"Clear the way, ladies," an EMS worker called from the door. After Alexandra and the others scooted out of the way, a gurney was carried down. A blood-soaked sheet covered a slim body. One bloodied arm, clad in lavender cashmere, dangled from under the sheet. Strands of thick blond hair draped over the end of the gurney.

Alexandra felt as if the ground had dropped out from underneath her. "Oh no. *No!*" she screamed. "Not Jessica!"

"No, not Jessica."

Gasping, Alexandra looked up. "Jessica!" she cried. "It wasn't you! Oh, thank goodness—"

"Alex, I don't know how to break this to you," Jessica interrupted, "but it was Susan."

"Susan?" Alexandra squeaked. "My little sister?"

"She's been murdered!" Caryn cried. "It just doesn't make any sense. Who'd want to kill Susan? She is the sweetest person I know . . . or she was." Caryn wailed. Denise wrapped her in her arms and stroked her hair soothingly.

As Alexandra looked around at all the girls in tears, panic grew inside her. Before she could speak, Alison Quinn shoved into their midst and grabbed Alexandra's arm.

"Oh, Alex, it's horrible. Your own little pledge sister!" Alison cried. "Stabbed to death right in our TV room."

"Who did it? Did they catch—"

"Some maniac killed her while we were all right here in the house." She glanced past Alexandra and waved her arms. "There's Tina! Tina! Did you hear? Someone killed Susan. . . ." Alison rushed away to spread the news like some demented town crier.

123

"I can't believe she's dead," Jessica said, dabbing at her runny mascara with a tissue. "Me, Izzy, and Lila were right here with Susan until about an hour ago. Yesterday Susan said how much she really liked my style, so this morning I fixed her hair just like mine. After the ceremony I loaned her my new lavender sweater, and then Izzy painted her nails to match." Jessica paused long enough to take a deep, quivering breath and wipe her eyes again. "I even loaned her the matching earrings."

"Lila's earrings," Isabella corrected.

As if she'd heard the mention of her name, Lila pushed her way into their huddle. "Jess," she whispered confidentially. "I just heard one of the cops tell one of the coroner guys that Susan's earrings are missing—that they'd been ripped right out of her ears." Lila illustrated with a dramatic yanking motion.

Alexandra's hands automatically jerked upward, as if to protect the tiny gold hoops she wore in her ears.

Lila began wringing her hands. "You don't think she was killed because of a robbery, do you? If she was, then it's almost like . . . like it's my fault. They were my earrings and everything. And they were *not* cheap. . . ."

"That couldn't have been it, Li. Don't blame yourself."

"No, I think it was. . . ."

"It had to be. . . ."

Suddenly it seemed as if everyone started talking at once—comforting, blaming, gossiping, expressing fear or theories. Alexandra couldn't sort out the words. She wondered if she was going into shock.

He actually did it, she thought with numbed amazement. *The crazed caller actually killed Susan. But why? To get my attention? No. This can't possibly have anything to do with me. It just can't!*

But deep inside, Alexandra knew better. The call. The warning. The murder. They'd all followed too closely to be coincidence. She was involved, and she had to tell the police.

She looked up at the wide-open door that led to the TV room. Policemen, both in uniform and plain clothes, bustled in and out, doing their jobs. One of them could help her. Protect her. Protect her sorority sisters.

"Excuse me, ladies." A policeman came down the steps, carrying an armload of evidence bags.

Grab him! Alexandra told herself. *Grab him and tell him what you know!*

Her arm rose, reached out, but then fell heavily to her side. She couldn't say anything to the police. If the caller found out she talked to the cops, he'd slice and dice her before sunset.

She gazed across the perfectly manicured lawn.

Yellow crime scene tape was draped around it like macabre party streamers. Just beyond, a large crowd of curious onlookers had gathered.

The killer could be there in that crowd. He could be that guy in the jogging suit . . . that guy in the Sigma sweatshirt. . . . He could be watching her this very minute. He'd know if Alexandra spilled to the police. And then she'd be next. . . .

Chapter Eight

I can't believe this is happening, Alexandra thought. *It's all too unreal.* The past two days had been a blur—a horrible foggy nightmare. And Sunday, as she stood in the dreary cemetery, watching Susan Zercher's coffin being lowered into the ground, she wasn't entirely sure she had awakened yet.

Sweet Rest Memorial Park would have been a perfect setting for one of those awful horror movies her neighbor Cheri watched. It was an old cemetery. The kind with huge ornamental headstones and sickly trees that seemed to be perpetually shedding leaves.

Even the weather had joined in to set a somber, dismal mood. It had been pouring rain all morning, but now the rain had slowed to a steady cold drizzle. Leaden clouds hung low, leaving everything in deep gray shadows, turning people into somber gray ghosts amid piles of sodden wet flowers.

As she shifted her weight from one tired leg to the other, Alexandra's black heels sank into the soft, wet ground. She stumbled slightly—not falling, but just wobbling enough to bump her umbrella into the umbrella next to her. "Excuse me," she whispered.

Kimberly Schyler, Theta treasurer, reached over and squeezed Alexandra's free hand in reply. Beyond her Denise stood with her boyfriend, Winston Egbert. Winston was so much taller than Denise, the umbrella that he so dutifully held wasn't doing Denise a bit of good. On Alexandra's other side Alison Quinn and Mandy Carmichael stood sharing an umbrella. Nearly all the Thetas, actives and pledges, had shown up. But they were only a small part of a very large gathering. Susan's family was at the center of the crowd, huddled together beneath a grungy green canvas awning that bore the name of the funeral home in giant white letters. If Alexandra stood on tiptoe, she could see Susan's mother leaning against her husband. Alexandra closed her eyes, not wanting to look anymore. And she didn't want to hear either—but she could. Mrs. Zercher's sobs were louder than the droning words of the funeral director.

The whole scene made Alexandra think of her

own mother. Her parents had been divorced since Alexandra was in junior high. *Who would Mom have to lean on if something happened to me?* she wondered. *And who would she miss—me or Enid?*

Alexandra clenched her jaw. She hadn't been home much since coming to college. Maybe she should go home for a visit soon and let her mother see how she'd changed. In fact, getting away from campus was sounding more and more like a very good thing—the sooner, the better.

"This is horrible," Alison sobbed next to her. "Such a waste!"

For once Alexandra agreed with something Alison said. The whole situation was a total tragedy. Tears ran down her cheeks as she remembered how friendly and energetic Susan had been. They had just become sorority sisters. Under normal circumstances, they should have had a chance to become friends for life. But for Susan life was over. It was so unfair!

And it's all my fault.

Closing her eyes again, Alexandra concentrated on the pattering sound of rainwater running off the funeral home's awning, hoping it might drown out the sniffling and sobbing sounds that surrounded her. When that didn't work, she tried focusing on the funeral director's words. . . . He was talking about peace, and love, and beauty. He hadn't mentioned a word about murder, or psychopaths, or the fact that Susan's life had been stolen.

Again Alexandra began to rake herself across the coals. *Why didn't I call someone immediately?* she asked herself. An oath of confidentiality didn't seem very important compared to someone's life. But how was she supposed to have known the crazy caller was serious? And how could she have known who he was after?

Why Susan? It didn't make any sense. If the guy was going to kill someone, some friend who was supposedly leading her astray—astray from *what,* she had no idea—then why would he go after someone she'd just met?

Logically there's no connection between my caller and Susan's murderer, she thought, grasping at anything that might make her feel better. *Maybe the motive for her murder was robbery, just as Lila suggested . . . and it had nothing to do with me.*

But she wasn't convinced. Somehow—even if she didn't understand why—she knew that Susan's death was her fault. The caller had warned her not to hang up, and she had. The caller had warned her not to tell anyone, and she hadn't—yet. But should she? He was still out there, waiting.

A chill skittered up her spine, and suddenly Alexandra remembered a silly old saying her grandmother used to say when she shivered:

"Somebody just ran across my grave." It had always sounded goofy when she was a kid, but now it sounded ominous. Was her caller out there, running across people's graves? Was he out there right now behind one of the large tombstones? Or even scarier, was he mixed in with the crowd of mourners, watching the service?

Her eyes scanned the crowd. Raincoats, umbrellas, hats over bent heads, tissues pressed over faces . . . How could she hope to recognize anyone?

She pushed that thought from her mind. She couldn't function if she convinced herself he was here now. If he was crazy enough to go around stabbing people, surely he couldn't just blend into a group of sane people.

As the crowd began to disperse, Alexandra realized that the services were over. Nervously she glanced around the cemetery. Her car was way down at the end of a long gravel drive. Why had she come to the funeral alone?

He's out there, she thought. *He wants to destroy me*. The cemetery suddenly seemed darker, and the many tombstones between her and her car suddenly seemed taller and more shadowy.

But surely I'm safe as long as I make it to my car while there are still people around, she told herself. Shivering more from fear than the cold rain, Alexandra hurried toward her car. *Nothing can happen to me in a crowd, can it?*

She reached out to open her car door. A strong hand closed around hers. She dropped her umbrella.

Noah jumped back as Alexandra shrieked. He hadn't meant to startle her, but he wanted to catch her before she got away.

"Your umbrella," he said. A gust of wind sent it windmilling away.

"I don't care," she said. "Let it go." With a weak little moan she sank against his chest.

Noah opened his raincoat and wrapped it around her as far as it would go. Without loosening his hold on her, he edged over slightly and leaned against her car. "Shhh . . . you'll be OK. I'm here now," he murmured against her soft, sweet-smelling hair. "Let it all out."

"Oh, Noah. I've been so miserable!" she cried. Despite the cold drizzle in his face he could feel her tears soaking through his shirt. "I'm so glad you're here. I was afraid—"

She squeezed him so tightly around the waist, he could hardly breathe, but he didn't complain.

"These past three days have been so horrible." She loosened her grip and raised up slightly to look at him. "I've missed you so. Why did we ever fight?" She dropped back against his shoulder and buried her face beneath his raincoat.

Noah rocked her gently and pressed his lips to her hair. He didn't dare say a word—not with the way their luck had been going lately. He was determined not to fight with Alexandra today, even if he had to stay as silent as a mime to do it. He loved her so much that he didn't care what he had to do to keep them together.

"Susan was so full of life. So bubbly. You never even met her, Noah, but she reminded me a lot of . . ." Alexandra's words trailed off as she gripped him tighter.

He wished they could stay like this forever. How perfectly she fit in his arms. How soft she was. How warm. He closed his eyes and breathed in the fresh, familiar scent of her perfume.

"It's all my fault," she sobbed.

Thinking she was talking about their last fight, he opened his mouth to disagree. But she rambled on, not making any sense.

"It's true. Just because of me—and she hardly even knew me, but she's dead just the same. How could I know it would happen, Noah? I didn't know."

She began to cry in loud, heartrending sobs. All he could do was hold her.

Suddenly he felt her grow stiff in his arms. As she began to pull away he fought back his instinctive urge to hold tighter, to not let her go.

She stepped back and looked up at him. Almost as if she'd pulled a mask over her face, her expression changed. She went from hysterical to blank in a fraction of a second. Wiping the tears and rain from her face with the back of her hand, she sniffed loudly.

"Noah. I'm sorry," she announced in a cold, perfectly modulated voice. "It's just not going to work between us."

"Alex!" He held up his hands in a hopeless gesture. "I didn't say a word!"

"I think we should break up," she continued. "Once and for all."

He couldn't believe his ears. "What are you talking about?"

"It's over. Just accept it." She turned away from him and opened the front door of her car.

It had happened. Just as he'd feared, Alexandra had come completely unglued. He leaned over the open door as she slipped into the driver's seat. "Alex. I know you're devastated about your friend, but we—"

"No. This has nothing to do with Susan. This is just between you and me. I've made my decision, so there's no use arguing. I think we should break up . . . completely."

He stared into her face, trying to seek out any hint of what she was feeling, but couldn't read a thing. Her eyes were as blank as her face.

"Alex, be reasonable. I know you're hurting, but why would that make you want to break up with me?"

"Because. I just do, that's why."

"This is childish. Give me one good reason."

"I'll give you a reason. The best reason. Because . . . I—I don't love you anymore."

If lightning had snaked out of the low black clouds and zapped him right in the chest, it couldn't have hurt more than Alexandra's words. He stared in disbelief. Although he'd feared Alexandra had been losing interest, he'd never dreamed she could stand there and so coldly tell him she didn't care.

"Alex, please. Don't do this. Don't push away the people who care about you."

"Leave me alone, Noah!" she shouted, then her voice dropped to hardly more than a whisper. "It's for your own sake."

"What?"

She yanked her hand away from his.

"Wait—I didn't catch that last part. Is this for my own sake? If that's what you said, that's a crock."

She fumbled for her keys, silent.

"It's nothing but a lame excuse! Listen to me! If we're breaking up for my sake, then we're not doing it. I don't want to lose you."

"I didn't say for your sake," she snapped. "I said you're a big *mistake*."

She started the car, but he refused to let go of the door. "Let me come with you. We can talk. I think I at least deserve a reason for getting dumped in the middle of a graveyard!"

"Move, Noah. I've got to get out of here."

He slammed his hand down on top of the car. The loud pop of bending metal was much louder than he'd expected. It caused them both to jump.

Alexandra reached for the door and pulled it. Noah jammed his hip in the way. Taking the weight of the door against the center of his back, he winced. Tears caused his vision to blur—but he wasn't sure if they were from pain or anger or both.

"*Move,* Noah!"

"OK! I'll back off," Noah agreed, his body and soul aching. "I'll give you room, but we aren't through. You mean too much for me to just let you walk out of my life without an explanation. I can't let you just throw it all away. I don't know what your problem is right now, but you'll come back to me."

"I don't want you to come near me!" she shouted, shoving him away from the car. "Stay away if you know what's good for you, Noah." Before he could regain his balance, she'd slammed the door and clicked the locks.

"I'm warning you, Alex," he shouted as she put the car in gear. He hit the window and grabbed at the handle. "If you keep shoving away the people who care about you, before long you won't have anybody."

But Alexandra never looked back. She just sped away, slinging mud over Noah's dress pants and leaving two wide ruts in the soft, muddy ground.

"This is far from over, Alex!" he hollered. The rain beating down mercilessly around him, he dropped to his knees in the mud and cried.

Alexandra was relieved to get back to her dorm room before Trina returned from her stay with her parents. Not only did she need some time alone, but Trina would have gone ballistic if she'd found out Alexandra left the door unlocked. But she had no choice. She still hadn't found her dorm keys.

She kicked off her muddy high heels and peeled off the damp black dress she'd worn to Susan's funeral. After slipping into an oversize gray sweat suit, she grabbed a towel and twisted it turban style around her hopelessly frizzy hair. Still she didn't feel warm. The wet and cold seemed to have seeped all the way to her bones. Shivering, she plopped onto her bed and bundled her comforter around her.

She'd never wanted a drink as badly as she did right now. She could almost feel the smooth, cool bottle in her hands, smell the sharp, familiar aroma, and taste the bitterness on her tongue. Her mouth watered just thinking about the oblivion that she could so easily hide in if only she had a drink. But her stash was long gone. She sighed, remembering all the booze she'd poured down the drain when she made the decision to quit.

I could run out to Beezers, she thought. *They never card there.* But the idea of going out didn't seem very appealing. Besides, deep down she knew that even if she were to drink herself into nothingness, tomorrow it would all be the same. Noah would still be angry with her. Susan would still be dead. And the killer would still be out there—waiting, watching her, calling her on the phone.

She glanced toward the phone, hating it for all the pain it had caused her lately. At the same time she remembered when it had been her friend. How she wished she could call the hot line like she used to in the old days, when Noah worked there. But somehow she didn't think that telling her troubles to Fred would have the same calming effect.

"I don't need a drink. I'm in control of my own life," she chanted, pulling the comforter more tightly around her shoulders. "Alcohol doesn't control me. I control it. I *choose* to stay in control . . . one day at a time." She took a deep breath, shut her eyes, and began again. "I don't need a drink. I'm in control of my own life. . . ."

But how can I control my own life when there's a nut out there with a knife, wanting to control it for me?

She flopped over on her pillow and looked up

at Noah's picture on her desk. She loved the way his smile was just a little bit crooked. Even from her upside-down viewpoint, he was handsome. In his picture he appeared to be so happy, but she knew that he wasn't—not now. Not after what she'd done. "Sorry to be so cruel," she said with a sigh. "But it *was* for your own good. I can't allow you to be seen with me—not as long as that nutcase is out there trying to kill off my friends."

Her abrupt breakup with Noah in the cemetery had been one more torture piled on top of everything else that had been happening lately. But it seemed like the only thing to do at the time.

For a few minutes there at the funeral, she'd almost convinced herself that there was no connection between the murder of Susan and her harassing caller. After all, even assuming that some crazed psycho wanted to scare her to death, and even assuming he was crazy enough to kill someone just to prove a point—wouldn't he have at least chosen someone close to her? A good friend or a boyfriend? It didn't follow that he'd kill someone she hardly knew.

The argument had sounded good. But while she was in Noah's arms, telling him about Susan . . . it had suddenly occurred to her how similar Susan and Jessica Wakefield were. Susan had hair the color of Jessica's, fixed like Jessica's. She'd been wearing Jessica's sweater. Susan and Jessica were approximately the same height and size. They were both bubbly and beautiful Thetas. Alexandra herself had even believed Jessica *had* been killed when she saw the body being carried out of Theta house.

Suddenly everything came into focus. What if the madman thought he was killing Jessica? The thought terrified her all over again—and refilled her with guilt. If this madman was after her friends, then who would be next? Trina? Noah? Isabella? Lila? Denise? She couldn't take any chances. She simply wouldn't have friends. Not if it meant putting them in danger.

Tears fell from her eyes. She *was* responsible for Susan's death. However indirectly it might have been—the guilt was still there, eating away at her. She couldn't allow herself—or anyone she knew—to be put in that same position again. But how could she stop it?

"Stay away from me, Noah," she told his picture. "For your own sake."

Sobbing uncontrollably, she rolled over and shoved her face deep into her pillow, not wanting her wails to be heard through the paper-thin walls. As Alexandra dug deeper into her covers and slipped her hands under her pillow something scratched her finger—something cold and hard.

With a sniff she wiped her eyes on the corner

of her comforter and picked up her pillow. There, pinned to her sheet, was the pledge pin she'd given Susan. Although all the pledge pins were similar, she recognized this one immediately. After all, it was the very same one her big sister, Magda Helperin, had given Alexandra when she was a pledge. With trembling fingers she unpinned it and held it up to the light to make doubly sure. There was the little scratch over the Alpha that she'd gotten one night when she had been drinking—she'd fallen against a brick planter at Zeta house.

"Susan would never have taken it off," she mused aloud. The killer had to have taken it from her.

But how did it get here?

Alexandra's heart literally stopped for a moment, then it began to pound ferociously. "He was here," she murmured. "He was here in *my room!*"

Alexandra rolled off the bed and climbed to her feet. Dragging the comforter with her, she ran to the door to make sure she'd locked it. On rubbery legs she wobbled as far as her desk chair before collapsing. She grabbed the phone, but as dizziness swept over her she let her fingers slide away.

He'll know. If I call the police, he'll somehow find out and come after me.

She leaned over and yanked the window shade closed.

He can't see me. I'm being silly. There's no way he could know.

Again Alexandra reached for the phone. This time she even got so far as to dial 911. But as the ring echoed in her ear she froze and slammed down the receiver.

What could she tell the police? She had no evidence. Not really. They could say that all pledge pins were alike. And even if she ignored her oath of confidentiality and confessed about the hot line calls, there would be no proof that anyone called her there; the hot line didn't log in or record calls. And if the maniac called from a campus phone, the phone company would have no record of it either.

"I don't have a shred of information the police could use," she whispered, panicking. "I don't know his name, or what he looks like, or where he lives or . . . anything. Except . . . except that he's demented."

She picked up Noah's picture and jumped back into her bed. "What can I do, Noah? Don't just sit there smiling. Help me out! Should I tell someone? Am I bound to keep this stuff secret just because it came over the hot line? It wasn't like he was asking for help or anything. He wasn't . . . confessing something."

Or was he?

Shaking her head fiercely, Alexandra pounded her bed with her fists. There was nothing she

142

could do. No way out. Nowhere to turn. And she was too confused and scared to think about it anymore. Clutching Noah's picture to her chest, she dropped back on her bed and cried.

The phone rang. The sound cut through her like a knife. She froze.

I can't answer it. I won't.

She stood up, wiped away her tears, and ripped the phone cord from the wall.

Chapter Nine

"Have you seen Alexandra?" Luke asked a group of students who were combing through a pile of glass bottles and jars, looking for ones they could use in art class.

Not getting the answer he wanted, he hitched up his jeans and climbed up a virtual hill of squashed cardboard boxes and looked around. He'd been looking for Alexandra ever since he'd arrived at the junkyard. She had to be here somewhere—it was a class requirement.

The minute Luke had heard that their class would be taking a field trip to the local junkyard to find stuff to incorporate into their sculptures, he had been excited. It sounded like the perfect opportunity for him to get closer to Alexandra—especially after she'd volunteered to drive. They'd all agreed to meet in the lobby of the art building at seven forty-five and depart at eight.

Luke had arrived at seven. He didn't want to take a chance on Alexandra's car being full before he got there. How did he know being overly punctual would get him stuck in Terry's minivan and running errands in the junkyard even before the majority of the class would arrive?

At last he spotted her coming across the desolate landscape with a canvas bag slung over her shoulder. Luke was alarmed at how awful Alexandra looked. Her jeans and baggy sweatshirt practically swallowed her. She had her hair pulled back in a severe ponytail, with a baseball cap stuck on top of that. It was almost as if she were trying to hide in her own clothes.

Luke waved and climbed down from his perch.

"I feel as if I'm on a scavenger hunt," Alexandra said as Luke fell into step beside her. Although she spoke brightly and smiled, her expression was tense and pained. She wasn't wearing a trace of makeup. Her face was pale except for the dark circles under her eyes and a smattering of freckles across the bridge of her nose. She looked so tired and discouraged, his heart went out to her. He wanted to help her any way he could.

"I've already found most of the junk on my list. Want some help with yours?" Luke offered.

Alexandra smiled weakly. "Sure, I'd appreciate it. Do you really think we'll find any of this stuff?"

"They've got everything here—even the kitchen sink," he joked, pointing to a shoulder-high mound of plumbing supplies.

She unfolded her list. "OK. I still need to find a plastic bucket, several large blocks of wood, some metal coat hangers—well, forget that one. I've got plenty of those in my dorm room."

"Let me see," Luke asked. He took her list, pulled his glasses from his pocket, and slipped them on. ". . . a large tin can—preferably one with a lid . . . a chair . . ."

"A chair! What are we going to do, make art or furnish Terry's apartment? Surely our kook of an art professor doesn't actually expect me to find a chair out here and drag it home."

"Actually, I know where some are." Luke pulled off his glasses and stuck them in his jacket pocket. "I saw them earlier. All kinds. A bunch of old recliners . . . bent metal chairs . . . wooden ones . . . This place is a virtual old-furniture grave-yard." Luke winced at his poor choice of words. "Sorry," he uttered, blushing in embarrassment.

"That's OK. Just a figure of speech, I know."

"But pretty insensitive of me. I heard about your friend's funeral," he said. "It was all over the *Gazette*. I'm really sorry."

Alexandra nodded but didn't speak.

Luke led her through a maze of sky-high, twisted scrap metal. Their apocalyptic surroundings seemed to suggest the aftermath of some bizarre disaster—a nuclear holocaust, a meteor strike—and he and Alexandra were the last two people left in the world. It wasn't the prettiest picture, but the idea of being so alone with Alexandra filled his heart with longing.

"I know how you must be feeling," he said softly. "A friend of mine died not too long ago. I know it sounds pretty lame, but if you need to talk or anything—"

Alexandra smiled sadly. "I could have used that offer yesterday. I spent most of the afternoon in my room talking to myself—" Suddenly she broke off as something seemed to catch her eye. "Listen, Luke." She pushed up the bill of her cap and yanked up her drooping sleeves. "You may think this sounds crazy, but I'm through making lopsided little bowls. I want to do something worthwhile for my class project."

Luke smiled. Alexandra suddenly looked so beautifully inspired; her face glowed and her eyes brightened. "Great. What?"

"I'm going to make a sculpture to memorialize Susan," she said decisively. "And I know the perfect place for it. There's this great little garden behind Theta house. You should see it. It's the most lovely, peaceful place. There are roses and little wrought iron benches."

"Wow, it sounds great. But what about your

memorial? What are you going to use?" He looked down at the pile of wood they'd just stepped over. "Wood?"

She shook her head.

"Terra-cotta? Ceramics? . . . Not scrap metal."

Alexandra chuckled. "No. I know I'm not a very advanced student, but I'm talking about something a little more daring. A really major sculpture. I want it to mean something."

"All right." Luke picked up a deflated basketball and juggled it between his hands. "Whatever it is, go for it. I'll be happy to help any way I can."

"I was hoping you'd say that." Taking his arm, she turned him toward a large muddy chunk of limestone. It looked as if it were about his height—maybe six feet tall or so. "I have a feeling I'm going to need a big strong man any minute now."

Her touch made him feel slightly dizzy. He chucked the basketball, grinned, and crooked his arm to show his muscles. "I offered, didn't I—but I'm not Popeye. So how about let's go see if they have a dolly back in the office."

Luke secured them a rusty old two-wheeler that was so beat-up, it probably should have been called a one-and-a-half wheeler. He coaxed the heavy chunk of limestone onto the dolly and helped Alexandra lug the stone across the junk-yard to the parking area. The morning sun shone down hard on him, and rivers of sweat were soon running down his back. With one last loud grunt he heaved the rock into her car. Even the car's shocks squeaked in protest. "Whew! That was heavy." He wiped sweat from his forehead with his sleeve. "But we did it."

"We did. Thanks, Luke." She favored him with a sad smile.

Luke's shoulders drooped. Alexandra's temporary excitement had vanished; she seemed to have sunk back into the sad figure who'd first arrived at the junkyard. Maybe he hadn't been much help after all. Or maybe that's all she wanted him for—his help. She already had a boyfriend. What did she need him for, really? He turned to walk away, dejected.

"Luke?"

He swung back around.

"I think I'm going to need a lot of help getting started on this project," she said. "See you in class tomorrow, OK?"

Luke's heart soared. Maybe he stood a chance after all.

Monday evening Alexandra had almost decided not to go in for her shift at the hot line. Her heart pounded frantically at the mere thought. She didn't want to risk getting another one of those terrifying calls again. But if she sat moping in her room for one more second, she thought she'd go crazy.

But after a few hours with no problems—and only one caller, who wanted to complain about her boyfriend's smoking—she relaxed. At least it had been a quiet night. One good thing about working at the hot line, when there were no callers, it was about the quietest place on campus—even better than the library for studying or doing homework. Alexandra had spent most of the past hour doodling sketches of her memorial sculpture ideas on a pad of art paper. She'd filled up nearly four pages, but so far none of the ideas had really grabbed her. She wanted it to be really special—maybe even spectacular. She flipped to a clean page and began sketching a face.

When the phone rang, she reached for it automatically. "Hello, SVU Substance Abuse Hot Line."

"Hello, my darling."

"I—I'm sorry," she stammered. "I think you have the wrong number."

She slammed down the phone. Shaking, she pushed away from her desk and hugged herself.

Fuming, he immediately hit the redial button. "Don't hang up on me again!"

"This is the SVU Substance Abuse Hot Line. Please check to see if you have dialed the right number."

"*I* know I have the right number, and *you*

150

know I have the right number! Listen, love. I know who you are. And you know who this is. Don't play games with me, Enid."

"Leave me alone!"

"I love the way you sound right now," he purred. "You're scared. I can hear it in your voice. And it *really* turns me on."

"You—"

"No. Don't try to deny it. It's OK. I know you're into it too."

"Shut your—"

"Oh, come on. You know you love it. Why aren't you hanging up on me, Enid?"

Silence.

"You can't hang up on me. Because you know what I'll do to you if you do." He stroked the handle of his hunting knife. It was clean, clean and perfect, freed of that manipulative little slut's blood. "I'm glad you're scared. And I want you to stay scared, Enid. That way I know you're paying attention. It means Alexandra is weakening and letting my Enid come through."

"Stop calling me Enid! That's not my name!"

"Ah, but we both know better, don't we, *Enid*. You're not Alexandra—not for much longer anyway."

"Shut *up!* Enid's *dead!*"

He clucked his tongue. "Oh, please. Enid's not dead. She's just tied up—hidden away in a little box somewhere. Somewhere inside you. And I'm going to set her free. . . ."

She gasped. Perfect.

He twirled the knife in the air. "And I'm going to *cut her out of you*."

"Don't you dare threaten—"

"It's not a threat, Enid. It's a promise."

More silence. Fast, shallow breaths. Faster. She was driving him crazy.

"Stop it, Enid," he moaned. "You're making me want to—"

"I'm hanging up."

"Don't you dare hang up on me!" he roared. "You need to listen to me. My love is the only thing that can save you from Alexandra's manipulation."

"You—you're not making sense."

"Don't you see? We're perfect for each other. It's destiny. Perfect pure love between people left behind. Society's rejects," he said with a sad sigh. "Travis and Enid, true love forever."

Her gasp was like a little hiccup. "Your name is . . . Travis?"

Travis flushed with rage and slammed his hand against the stucco wall. How could he have been so stupid? He'd hidden his name for so long!

But as suddenly as his fury rose, it ebbed away. He wiped a hand roughly across his face and laughed. What did it matter? She would have to know his name eventually. She might as well know it now.

"Nice name, isn't it?" he asked. "But don't bother running to the police with it, Enid love. They'd never figure out who I am. Only you know about me. Otherwise . . . I don't even exist. But I'm here for you, Enid. Don't worry. Whenever you need me, I'll know because I'm watching you. I'm here waiting. Right under your pretty little nose, practically."

"Travis isn't your real name?"

"Of course it is. I'm really Travis . . . just like you're really Enid. It's my *real* name. It's who I am. I'm not pretending like you are."

"But who—"

"Don't be so impatient. You'll know me soon enough. When the time is right for me to show you my love . . . I'll reveal myself to you."

"Stop it!" she screamed. "You're completely psycho! I don't know you. I don't love you. I *hate* you. You're a cold-blooded killer, you freak!"

"You don't hate me," he said coldly.

"I've never hated anyone so much in my whole life. You *disgust* me."

He could feel the muscles of his neck bunching up. His head was starting to ache. This call had started out so beautifully. Now it wasn't going well at all. He felt sick; sick and disappointed with his Enid. She wasn't making him very happy. She needed to be taught another lesson.

"Maybe you feel that way right now, my love," he said, dropping his voice to a low growl. "But as they say in all those silly little psychology books, there's a fine line between love and hate. Soon you'll cross that line. Soon we'll both cross that line."

Travis slammed the phone down as hard as he could. This time he'd let *her* see how it felt to be hung up on.

Alexandra gripped the receiver so tightly, her knuckles whitened. It felt like a snake—a snake she'd caught right behind its head. If she let go, it would bite her.

When the wailing, buzzing off-the-hook siren erupted, it startled her so much, she dropped the phone. She quickly picked it back up, but her hand was shaking so badly, it took her two tries to set the receiver back in its cradle.

She put her head between her knees and tried to breathe. The way her whole body was twitching and trembling reminded her of a rabbit she'd had once when she was a little girl.

Rabbit? Alexandra looked at herself. She was hunkered down and quivering like a frightened rabbit, ready to run. The caller was right. She *was* turning back into Enid!

She took a deep breath and began counting slowly. Just when her pulse lowered back down, she heard the lock on the office door click. She screamed and jumped under her desk.

A creak, then footsteps. Alexandra held her breath. The footsteps became louder. She spotted a pair of sneakers from under the desk. She trembled and closed her eyes, waiting for Travis to find her and—

"Hey, is anyone *working* here?"

Alexandra popped her head up. "F-Fred?"

Fred tilted his head to the side and squinted at her. "What's with you, Enid?"

"Enid?" she screamed.

"Hey! I'm sorry, *Alexandra*." Fred shook his head. "What the hell are you doing under your desk?"

She gulped. "You . . . scared me."

"You? Scared of me? Oh, please." He laughed. "Get up, Alex."

She shakily got to her feet and arranged herself in her chair.

"You don't look so hot," he observed. "Are you on something?"

"What?" Alexandra cried. "No!"

"Well, you look pretty strung out." He paced around the office like an angry red-haired panther. "Maybe you were doing something *else* you weren't supposed to be doing—like taking personal phone calls, perhaps? I've warned you about that once, Alex. Don't make me warn you again."

Alexandra took hold of the edge of the desk to steady her shaking hands. Maybe she could talk to Fred about the caller. After all, he was supposed to be the hot line's adviser. Why not let him make the big decision about Travis—or whatever the guy's real name was. It was worth a try. Travis probably wouldn't find out about it. And it wasn't as if she would be going to the police or anything. In a weird way she'd be following Travis's rules— even though it sickened her to realize she was obeying him.

"Fred, can . . . can I talk to you about something?"

He narrowed his beady eyes suspiciously but didn't say no.

"I—I have a problem here at the hot line. There's this caller who said—"

"You shouldn't be telling me what a caller said, Alex," Fred said, his voice deep and serious.

"Well, normally I wouldn't, but I'm worried about—"

"Confidentiality is our number-one policy. We don't talk about what's said over the hot line. Not even to each other."

"It's the *policy* that I want to talk about. I'm not so sure—"

"Well, isn't that a coincidence?" He rubbed his

hands together joyfully. "This is *so* cool! You'll never guess where I've been." He paused, as if his statement held the mystery of the Sphinx.

Alexandra sighed in frustration. "Where, Fred?"

"The copy center."

Big whoop, she replied silently.

"In anticipation of a situation just like this one," he continued, "I ran off copies of our hot line policy." He disappeared through the door and reappeared waving a sheaf of shamrock green flyers.

"What do we need those for?" Alexandra asked.

"You know, I pride myself on my ability to read people," Fred intoned as if he hadn't even heard her. "It's a handy trait for anyone in managerial positions. I just knew Doug was the type to have wishy-washy rules." He handed her the first copy off the stack.

Alexandra glowered. She hated hearing that power-hungry creep bash Doug. And she *really* hated to think what Fred probably said about her behind her back. "Doug ran a tight ship," she countered. "He was not wishy-washy. And he was actually pretty *nice.*"

"What a shame," Fred went on. "It's tough working where policies aren't clear. But I don't think you'll have any problems interpreting *my* rules."

He reached over her head and tacked a green

sheet to the bulletin board. His ten rules were numbered in fancy Roman numerals. It somehow reminded her of the Ten Commandments. Although they weren't etched in stone and didn't start out with "Thou shalt not," Fred seemed to think they were just as important. He taped a copy over each phone, one beside the bathroom mirror, and yet another one on the back of the door.

"I have more copies if you need them," he offered.

"Um . . . I think we already have enough around the office, thanks," she quipped. "Unless you'd like me to hang one up in my dorm room too."

Fred scratched his scrawny little goatee as if lost in thought. "Hmmm . . . maybe that would be a good idea."

Alexandra rolled her eyes and stared at the paper in her hand. In bold capital letters number one leaped off the page:

1. ABOVE ALL ELSE, TOTAL CONFIDENTIALITY MUST BE MAINTAINED.

"Fred? I don't . . ."

"Got a problem with the rules?" he challenged, hands balled into fists on his hips.

"Well, about number one," she began. "Confidentiality. What if I knew something really important? Like, let's say—"

"No, let's *don't* say." Fred smacked his extra

copies against his open hand. "What word isn't clear to you, Alex? Is the word *confidentiality* too long for you to comprehend? It means that you don't tell anyone a word of what you've heard over the line. No exceptions. You don't breathe a word to *anyone*—not to me, not to your mama, not to your boyfriend, not to your dog. Nobody!"

"But why bring these in here now?" Alexandra cried. She wadded her copy of the rules into a ball and tossed it beside the phone.

Fred's eyes widened. "Hey, that copy cost me five cents!"

She choked back a frustrated scream.

"Look, Alexandra. It sounds to me like you're pretty confused about the hot line rules. Am I right?"

She shook her head. "You're not hearing me at all, Fred."

"Don't try to deny it. You know you're confused."

Alexandra squinted. Something about what Fred just said sounded so familiar. . . .

"Well, then, it's understandable to think that others might be too, isn't it?" Fred continued. "It's tough sometimes when a new person takes over. Things change. As a rule, people don't like change. But change can be a good thing. You probably know that better than anyone, Enid Alexandra Rollins."

She held her breath. Her heart pounded so loudly, she was sure Fred could hear it. No. He couldn't be—

"My policies are simple." He handed her another copy of the rules. "Here they are, clear and concise. No exceptions. I don't believe rules can be bent. They can only be broken. And that's one thing I won't abide. Do you hear me? I won't abide you telling *anyone* about *any* of the calls you receive. Are we clear on this?"

Alexandra gulped. "Wh-Why don't you trust me anymore?"

"Don't you think I trust you?" Fred asked with a chuckle. "If that's what you think, then I'd say you're getting a little bit paranoid. These rules are for everyone who works at the hot line. Do you see 'Dear Alexandra' typed at the top of this sheet? No. And I don't think I see 'Dear Enid' either." He laughed. "I don't think I should have to address you . . . sorry. I mean *both* of you."

Alexandra's breath caught in her throat. Fred's laugh. It sounded familiar, yes. But had she heard it on the phone? Or just here in the office? She didn't know anymore. . . .

She looked closely at Fred's arrogant, smug smile and mangy little goatee. Today he was wearing jeans, but he still looked stiff and pompous. He probably stayed home nights starching them and ironing a crease into them. Just what did he do outside of the office anyway? He seemed to be running in and out a lot, as if he had a lot of things to do—

Oh no. She gulped and desperately hoped her alarm wasn't showing on her face. Every time Travis had called, she had been alone in the office. In fact, if she remembered correctly, Travis had always called right after Fred left the office . . . and tonight, right before he came in.

Her stomach somersaulted. Not taking her eyes from him, she scooted as far away from Fred as the tiny room would allow.

Fred didn't seem to notice. He grinned toothily and scratched his goatee again as if it itched. "Well, now we've got that settled," he said calmly. "I've got places to go and people to see. You do plan to stay until eight, don't you? Or do you think you'll have another emergency come up at the sorority house?" He laughed scornfully. It didn't sound scary—just annoying. The sound didn't ring any bells with her. Then again, his voice didn't either. . . .

Stop it! she told herself. *You're just overreacting. You're just imagining things. Sure, Fred is arrogant, overbearing, and egotistical. He's a total jerk. But that doesn't make him a psycho murderer.*

Does it?

161

Chapter Ten

"Is this how you want it?" Luke groaned from the strain as he helped Alexandra pull the heavy limestone slab to an upright position in the corner of the studio. Tuesday morning sunshine streamed in through a nearby dusty window.

"Thanks, Luke," she said with a toss of her shimmering copper waves. "I don't know what I'd have done without you. You're really strong."

He blushed and dusted off his hands on the seat of his jeans. "I lift weights every once in a while. It helped me get over my drinking problems. You know how it is."

Alexandra nodded. "I'll bet your art helps too."

"Yeah, it really does. But one person can only fit so many watercolors on one dorm-room wall. If I don't learn to control myself soon, I'm going to have to move to a bigger place."

The smile Alexandra flashed nearly floored him. A smile like that would make joking about any problem worthwhile, he thought.

"So, have you ever worked with limestone?" he asked, laying out a hammer, chisel, and polishing cloth for her.

She shook her head. "I'm crazy, aren't I?"

"I don't think so," he said, his heart swelling with admiration. He desperately wished he could tell her how moved he was by her decision to memorialize her friend with a sculpture. But he didn't want to scare her away. "I . . . I think it's really great what you're doing."

"Thanks," she said quietly. "I don't know—I really want to do something big, but I have a feeling I'm out of my league here."

"Not at all," Luke said with a grin. "We all have to start somewhere. But hey, you have something in mind, right? Some kind of plan—you know, an artist's vision?"

She looked at him, her green eyes wide—a little wary. "You aren't teasing me, are you?"

"Of course not," he said gently. "Look. Don't be afraid of the stone. What can it hurt? It's just a big rock. If you mess up, we'll just find you another one."

Alexandra went to her book bag and pulled out a slightly wrinkled sheet of art paper. She seemed almost afraid to show it to him. "Well, here's my idea. But . . . oh, you'll probably think it's stupid."

Luke's breath caught in his throat. "No, Alexandra," he insisted. "I'd really like to see it. I'd . . . I'd be honored."

"You're just being nice," she said, shaking her head shyly. "You're such a good artist, Luke. I bet you'll hate it."

"I won't." He crossed his heart. "I promise."

She looked at the paper, then back at him. "OK, I trust you." Nervously she walked over to him and handed him the paper. Her fingers brushed his for a moment, and his spine tingled. "Tell me what you think. But don't be mean."

"I'd never do that." Luke put on his glasses and examined the sketch. He saw a dark block with a roughly hewn blob on top of it. There were two points coming out of the blob, and something that looked like a face. He couldn't quite make out what it was supposed to be, but he didn't dare tell her that. He pointed to the dark blob. "This is the base, right?" he asked carefully.

"Right," Alexandra said brightly. "That'll be a clay pedestal for the memorial to sit on. That's where I'll put the inscription and maybe the Theta letters."

While Luke examined the sketch, she went back to the stone and ran her hands over the top. "This stone is going to be the centerpiece of the memorial. I want it to sit high on the pedestal, up off the ground so people can see it."

She glanced up as if she wanted his approval, so he nodded and set her paper down. "Go ahead," he urged. "Tell me exactly what you want it to be like."

"I want to carve a face—probably high relief, you know, just like half a face coming up from the stone. I'd like to make it real smooth and leave the rest of the stone rough, sort of like that slide we saw the other day."

"Rodin's *Danaïde*?"

"Yes. That's the one." She stroked the sides of the stone. "And then along here—I'm not positive yet—but I think I want wings. Maybe in low relief."

"Wings? Like a bird?"

"No. Like angel wings. Maybe it's corny, but that's how I picture Susan, as an angel."

Luke nodded. "Perfect. The way I see it . . ." He picked up a pencil and made a few light marks on the stone. "You can start about here with the tip of the wings and come along here, shaping them outward. . . ." Suddenly he stopped himself and stepped aside, blushing. "Sorry. I got carried away. It's your project."

"No, please, go on." She pushed a strand of hair away from her face. "I'm going to need all the help I can get."

"Well, if you're sure you don't mind."

Alexandra's smile was all the encouragement he needed. "You'll do most of your subtracting here," he began. "Making the wings seem as if they're folded behind her, like so. I'd start the face about here."

"Oh, wow!" she said. "That's exactly what I had in mind, but I didn't think I could do it."

"Well, just remember—the stone has the figure in it. It's just up to you to free it."

"So do you really think this stone has an angel in it?"

"You can only chip away at this rock awhile and find out."

"Well . . ." Her brow creased, those cute worry lines reappearing once again. "I'm sorry. I don't want to be a pain, and I know you're really busy, but . . . I could really use your help if that's OK. I know I'm not good enough to do a face."

"You can do it, Alexandra," he told her, wishing he could grip her by the shoulders and look deeply into her eyes—and not scare her away. "You may not have a lot of experience, but art comes from the heart. If you really believe in yourself and in what you're doing, the skill will come. And I know how strongly you feel about—"

Luke broke off and fanned his face with his hands. "Whew! Is it hot in here or is it just me?" He walked over to the windows and threw one wide open. He stood there long enough for his blush to subside. He couldn't imagine how he could have let himself go on and on like that to Alexandra. But she was so easy to talk to!

"Hey," she called gently. "Are you OK?"

"Yeah. Fine." He wanted to kick himself, but at least his face felt cooler. Taking a deep breath, he returned to her side. "I think you've got quite a project here."

She rocked back and forth on her heels nervously. "I know, but I really want to do it. Do you think I'm taking on too much?"

"No." He touched her shoulder, and she didn't move away. "I think it'll be beautiful, Alexandra. It's going to be quite a moving tribute when you're finished carving it."

"You are going to help me with it, aren't you?"

"Sure, I'll do whatever you want. Just ask." He dared to squeeze her shoulder, just lightly.

"OK." She stepped away, and for a moment Luke feared he had gone too far. But she simply picked up the chisel from the table and positioned it delicately toward the stone. With her other hand she lifted the hammer. "Now what?" she asked with a laugh.

Blushing again, Luke reached over and laid his hand over hers, changing the angle of the chisel. Her hand seemed so small in his. Warm and soft. "OK," he said, getting ahold of himself. "Whack it!"

Alexandra barely touched the small hammer to the end of the chisel.

Luke laughed. "That's a whack? C'mon, hit it hard!"

When she turned to look at him, her hair brushed against his face. It smelled like fresh apples. "But what if I hit your hand?" she asked, her face pinched with worry.

"You won't hit my hand," he said, gazing into her green eyes. "Just hit the end of the chisel."

"But what if I miss?"

"Then I'll yell like crazy."

Alexandra giggled and hit the chisel, harder this time. A chip of rock shot off in Luke's direction. He ducked.

"Sorry!" she cried, biting her lip. "Are you OK?"

"Not a scratch." Reluctantly he let go of her hand and stepped back. "So now you should just keep doing that . . . for a few hours."

"Oh, jeez." She wiped her forehead with her sleeve and let out a long, slow breath. "Well . . . I guess I'll get started, then." She held his gaze for a moment, then turned back to the stone.

"OK. Good luck." He walked away, but something compelled him to looked back over his shoulder.

She had been watching him. When he caught her staring, she hastily looked away. Luke felt his face redden, and he wobbled slightly. Pulling himself together, he said, "I'll be right over here if you need me."

Alexandra turned around and smiled. "Thanks, Luke. I really appreciate it."

He pulled down his bust from the shelf, set it on his worktable, and removed the wet towel. He felt a little strange. There stood Alexandra, chopping away at an immense rock to memorialize her dead friend, and there he sat, sculpting a stupid little bust of himself. Well, it was a requirement; he couldn't help it. But the selflessness of her art and the selfishness of his made him feel totally unworthy of her. With a long sigh he began refining the cheekbones, the sound of chisel against stone providing the sound track to his work.

"Luke, can I ask you something?"

He looked up from his project and took off his glasses. "Sure." Automatically he walked to the sink and began cleaning his hands. He didn't want to get clay on her sculpture.

"Um, it's not about art," she said. "It's sort of . . . personal, actually. A moral dilemma." She laughed shakily. "I'm sorry. I'm not bugging you, am I?"

"Not at all." Luke dried his hands and leaned back against the sink. Something personal? He couldn't believe she wanted to talk to him, confide in him—not like a classmate, but like a friend.

A moral dilemma—maybe it was something about her boyfriend. He ran a hand through his hair and tried to look as calm as possible. "You can ask me anything, Alexandra. Anything you want."

She put down the chisel and hammer and wiped her brow. "What do you think about rules?"

"I think they can be a pain in the butt," he said with a grin. "But they're necessary, I guess."

"You already know I work at the hot line, so I guess it's all right for me to tell you this." Alexandra took a deep breath. "In order to work there, we have to take an oath of confidentiality. It's really strict. We're not supposed to discuss anything anyone tells us with anyone for *any* reason. Do you think that's a good idea?"

Luke scowled, and he felt perspiration break out across his top lip. Quickly he reached up and wiped it away. "Why are you asking me?" he asked with a nervous laugh. "Does this have to do with my call?"

"It doesn't—"

"I bet it does." His eyes widened, and he wrung his hands. "You probably have to report me or something because I let you know who I was after I called, right? I broke the rules, and now I'm going to get in trouble."

Alexandra held out her hands and approached him. "Luke, calm down. It's not—"

"Oh, man." He turned around and clutched the edges of the sink with both hands. "I could get kicked out of the dorm if anyone found out about my drinking, not to mention what my mother would do!" He spun around, his face tight with anxiety. "You don't know my mother, Alexandra. She'd go ballistic if she thought I'd even *tasted* alcohol. Because of my dad—well, she's like a modern-day Carry Nation. She'd swing her hatchet at anything stronger than coffee!"

Alexandra laid her soft, pale hand on his arm. The light pressure of her fingers soothed him. "I'm sorry, Luke. I wasn't talking about reporting you," she said reassuringly. "Really. My mind was somewhere else entirely. I'm just saying, what do you think about the importance of sticking to a rule like that no matter what?"

He gulped. "I'm not sure what you're getting at," he said. "The whole reason I called the hot line was to get help—but I also knew my secret would be kept secret, you know?"

"Well, you know what they say—every rule has exceptions." Alexandra rubbed his arm for a moment, then stepped away, lost in thought. "I guess I'm not being clear enough. Let's say, for instance, someone called who was dealing drugs, not doing drugs. And maybe . . . maybe one of their clients OD'd."

Luke relaxed somewhat and busied his hands by rolling a ball of clay into a coil. "I don't know. Maybe. But who's to say what's OK to reveal and what's not? You might feel strongly that it's your duty to report something like that, but the next guy might feel just as strongly that he's justified in reporting someone *using* drugs to the police. You know, get them busted and put in jail rather than getting them help."

After a long pause Alexandra nodded. "That's a good point."

"Maybe it's just my personal opinion, but what's the use of having a confidential hot line if the volunteers might decide to narc on someone?" he asked. "Even if something awful came out of someone's confession, something criminal, it shouldn't be your job to put them in jail, you know what I mean? That's the police's job. You're there to help people, not get people in trouble. Even people who deserve it."

"I was afraid you'd say something like that." Alexandra picked up a ball of clay and rolled it nervously between her hands.

"Sorry." Luke shrugged. "I guess I wasn't very helpful."

"Don't be sorry." She looked up and gave him a weak smile. "I've been telling myself the exact same thing. I guess I just needed someone else's opinion."

"Well, if you wanted me to change your mind, I'm sorry I can't," he said sincerely. "I would never have been able to call the hot line before if I hadn't been certain no one would ever know who I was or what my problem was. I mean, it's OK that you recognized my voice. I know you won't rat on me, but . . ."

She set down the ball of clay and stroked his arm with the back of her hand. "I'm glad you trust me, Luke. I'd never betray that trust. What I said before—it doesn't really mean anything. It's just something that's been bugging me lately, that's all."

"It's OK," he said warmly. "I trust you. I really do."

Her smile sent a warm rush through his chest. How he wished he could just open his mouth and substitute the word *love* for *trust*. If he trusted himself, he would have.

As darkness settled over the campus Travis could see his reflection in his dorm-room window.

"Hurry up. You're running out of time," the reflection reminded him.

"I am hurrying," Travis replied. His fingers flew across the clicking, clacking keyboard. "But I have to get this just right. This note to Enid has to be absolutely perfect."

"Give her an ultimatum," the reflection demanded.

"No! I can't treat my Enid like that." Travis frowned, hit delete, and started typing again.

"There!" he said, smiling with satisfaction. "That's better. This will do the job!" He reached across his roommate's desk and switched on the printer.

As the printer began to hum and suck paper through the tractor feed Travis rubbed his hands together. How would Enid react when she got his note? He had a gut feeling that he hadn't quite gotten through to her about this whole confidentiality thing. He was certain this little surprise would convince her to keep her mouth shut.

Not that it really mattered if she went to the cops. They'd never believe her. And even if they did, the fools would never find him.

Travis imagined a whole troop of uniformed policemen going from dorm room to dorm room looking for a mysterious student named Travis. No telling how many Travises they'd root out. SVU was no small place. There had to be scads of Travises on campus. But none of them was him.

"Perfect!" he cheered. Travis and his reflection threw back their heads and laughed. But Travis stopped abruptly as another thought occurred to him.

"Even if they can't find me, I still don't need a bunch of cops hanging around campus," he said. "How can I get to Enid if cops are crawling all over the place?"

"They can't stop you," his reflection told him.

"You're absolutely right," he replied. "But they could make it harder for me to reach her. I have to get to her!" He slammed his fist against the desktop. "No one's going to interfere with my plans. No one's going to spoil this meeting for me. Soon I will be with Enid—cops or no cops."

"Then go get her," his reflection said.

"I will, but when the time is right . . . and when that time comes, it'll be such a waste of time, having to work around stupid cops."

"Don't get ahead of yourself, Travis," his reflection urged. "Take it one problem at a time. If the cops come, you can deal with them."

Travis's blood boiled. He didn't want to be reminded of the possibility. "Quiet!" he shouted at his reflection. He yanked the cord, dropping the window blinds into place. He was once again alone.

The printer beeped, reminding him that his note was waiting. Humming a catchy little tune, he leaned over and ripped the paper from the machine.

He wasn't worried about cops—not really. He would deal with anybody who tried to come between him and Enid. Police, sorority chicks, teachers, whoever—they were all vermin to him. Rats. Roaches. They needed to be exterminated.

Taking out his knife to cut off a strip of ribbon,

he broke out singing his own version of a tune he'd learned in kindergarten. "Five little rats outside the door; I stab one, then there's four."

He wound the ribbon into a large red bow. "Four sorority rats take my love from me. I kill one, then there's three. Three little rats dancing round my bed. I stab one, then she is dead. . . ."

He reread the note. "Perfect!" he proclaimed. He folded it carefully into a perfect little square and tucked it into the top of the white cardboard box where he had put the lovely keepsakes he'd been saving for the right moment.

"*This* will convince her that my intentions are oh so sincere." He slapped the bloodred bow on top of the box and taped down the lid. "A present for you, Enid. With love from Travis."

Chapter Eleven

"What? Who? . . ." Disoriented and groggy, Trina stirred against her pillow. Normally a sound sleeper, something had disturbed her, frightened her. She pressed her hands over her ears. At first she thought it was Cheri next door, watching those awful slasher movies she was addicted to . . . but it wasn't. Suddenly she sat bolt upright and stared at her roommate.

Across the room Alexandra, her face a mask of horror, was shrieking like a blond bimbo in a B movie. In one hand she held a small white gift box and in the other a creased sheet of paper.

Trina's blankets tangled around her legs, nearly tripping her as she tried to get from her bed to Alexandra's. "Alex, Alex! What is it?" She placed her hands on Alexandra's shoulders and shook her gently. "I'm here. It's OK. Calm down and tell me what's the matter."

Alexandra shook her head, and although her screams had stopped, her rasping breaths were almost as noisy.

"What's wrong?" Trina asked.

But Alexandra kept on gasping like a fish out of water. Her glassy eyes weren't focusing on Trina at all.

Trina snatched the note from her hand and read:

Just for you, my dearest Enid. Two beautiful little tokens of my esteem. Only you are worthy of these gifts. Remember, our special love is our little secret. *Keep it that way!*

Love eternally,
Travis

"Who's Travis?" Trina demanded, waving the note in her roommate's face. "What's this all about?" Trina practically climbed into Alexandra's lap. "Answer me, Alex. What's got you so upset?"

Alexandra began to rock back and forth on the bed. Without a word of explanation she passed the white gift box to Trina.

Trina's hand flew to her mouth and her stomach lurched violently. Inside the box two bloodied amethyst earrings glimmered dully on a bed of soft white cotton. What was that clinging to them?

Skin? She looked questioningly at Alexandra.

"Lila's earrings," Alexandra said flatly. She hugged her knees to her chest and kept rocking. "Susan was . . . wearing them . . . when . . . she was . . . killed."

Trina slapped the lid on the horrible box and threw it onto the floor. "Where'd you get that thing?"

"Here."

"What do you mean, here?"

"Here," Alexandra yelled, beating her hand against her comforter. "The box was lying right here at the foot of my bed when I woke up."

"It couldn't have just appeared here—not in our room. How could someone get in here if the door is locked?"

Tears rolled silently down Alexandra's pale face. Her whole body was shaking. "He was in our room again."

"Again? Who was?" Trina caught her arm and squeezed. "Who? This Travis? Who is he, Alex?"

"The killer. He killed Susan."

"I'm calling the police," Trina said, jumping up from the bed.

"No. Wait."

Trina couldn't believe her ears. "Wait? Some deranged killer has been creeping around in our room while we sleep, and you say *wait*? Alex, I've never been so terrified in all my life! We *have* to call the police."

Alexandra grabbed Trina's hands and gave her a pleading look. "We can't call the police, Trina. He'll *know*. Travis . . . the killer . . . he's watching us." As if the idea had just occurred to her, Alexandra dropped Trina's hand, hurried over to the window, and yanked the curtains closed.

"Alex, how could somebody be watching us? We're on the fourth floor."

"Don't you see?" Alexandra said, returning to Trina's side. "That's what this hideous thing is about." She snatched up the note and wadded it into a ball. "He's warning me that if I go to the police, he'll come after me next—or another of my friends."

Trina shivered, and the blood drained from her face. "Alex, we have to do something! He might come after us anyway!"

Alexandra wiped away her tears. She sucked in a deep breath and let it out noisily through her mouth. "You're right," she said, sinking back down on the bed. "If you'll hand me the phone, I'll call the police right now."

With trembling fingers Trina grabbed the phone and shoved it into Alexandra's lap. "Hurry, Alex. Hurry!"

*　　　*　　　*

Alexandra had to tell her story three different times before she was ever connected to Detective Bart Kaydon, the homicide detective who was in charge of Susan's murder case. And even he was skeptical.

As he began offering lame excuses Alexandra glanced over at Trina and rolled her eyes. Trina, who sat cross-legged on her bed, seemed to sink deeper into the huge floral comforter that engulfed her elfin little body.

"Let me assure you, Miss Rollins, we will definitely look into this," his nasal voice blared over the phone. "But quite frankly, we've had hundreds of calls from girls on campus this past week. Ever since the murder every noise in the night has sent some terrified coed to the phone."

Alexandra groaned with frustration. "But I *recognize* these earrings—"

"Yes, the earrings." Detective Kaydon cleared his throat. "I'll bet you have a boyfriend, don't you, Miss Rollins?"

"Yes, but—"

"Have you talked to him this morning? Maybe he sent you some earrings like the ones your friend had."

"Covered in blood? I don't think so!"

"Miss Rollins, please calm down."

"*Nobody* sent these earrings to me! Someone *left* them here—right in my room. And I'm telling you, these are the *exact* earrings that Susan Zercher was wearing when she was killed. Can't you guys analyze them for blood samples or skin tissues or something like that?"

Detective Kaydon sighed. "OK, Miss Rollins. If what you say is true and these earrings really did belong to the victim, they could be very important—the only lead we've gotten so far. How about if I have an officer stop by your dorm and pick them up?"

"No!"

Trina jumped up in alarm, but Alexandra waved her back down. She pressed her hand against her chest and answered more calmly. "I mean . . . that might not be a good idea. I'm pretty sure this guy is watching my room. If he sees a policeman, he might do something drastic. My roommate and I could be in real danger."

"Well, how about if I send a plainclothes officer? Would that make you feel better?"

"I—I don't know. . . ."

"My men are the best, Miss Rollins. I'll send someone who'll blend right in. If anyone is watching your room, they'll just see a guy who looks like an ordinary college student stopping by for a visit."

"But how will I know . . . ?"

"He'll have ID. And you shouldn't be afraid to ask to see it. OK?" Without waiting for her to answer, he continued, "Hang on a minute and I'll see who's available." Canned music began to buzz in her ear.

"I'm on hold again," Alexandra whispered, pressing her hand over the mouthpiece.

"What did he say?" Trina asked, hurrying over to her side.

"I think he's going to send someone over."

"You didn't tell them about the note. Don't you think you . . ."

Alexandra waved her away as Detective Kaydon's voice came back on the line.

"I don't have anyone free at the moment, Miss Rollins, but I'll round up someone as soon as I can. In the meantime you and your roommate sit tight. Don't go out alone, and don't let anyone in your room that you don't know."

"Yes, sir."

"When the officer gets there, give him the earrings. And if you've remembered anything—any information that's a little more concrete than what you've already told me—you might want to make a statement at that time. You really haven't given us much to go on."

Alexandra winced guiltily. Admittedly she hadn't told him everything, but she was still debating with herself exactly how much she could reveal about the hot line. And she didn't see any sense in telling him the murderer's name was Travis. She was sure it was a made-up name anyway.

"As I said, it's probably nothing to worry about," Detective Kaydon continued. "Most likely a fraternity prank. Those guys do some pretty disgusting things sometimes in the name of fun."

"What's he saying?" Trina asked again.

"He thinks it's a fraternity prank," Alexandra whispered.

"Yeah, right. Like frat boys have added ritual murder to their hazing schedules." Trina fell back on the bed. "That's a new one on me. Gee, thanks, Detective, I feel a hell of a lot better."

Alexandra touched her finger to her lips. Detective Kaydon was still talking.

". . . but it's better not to take chances. Until the guy who killed Susan Zercher is caught, just keep your eyes open and be careful. And he will be caught. Eventually this guy will make a stupid mistake. That's when we'll nab him."

"All right."

"In the meantime, I'll call your housing office and make sure they send someone to change your lock. I'll bet whoever played this prank has his hands on your lost keys."

"That would be great." Alexandra sighed. "Thank you, Detective Kaydon."

Although Detective Kaydon's skepticism annoyed her, Alexandra felt better while she was talking to him. Safer somehow. If nothing else, it helped to unload a little of the responsibility she'd been carrying all alone on her tired shoulders. But the moment she hung up the phone, she was overwhelmed by a deeply creepy sensation.

"Trina," she said quietly. "I think I've just made a really *big* mistake."

When the phone rang, she nearly jumped out of her skin.

Finally it's ringing! Travis thought as he slipped quietly out of the utility closet on the fourth floor of Parker Hall. That constant busy signal nearly drove him insane.

The hallway was deserted. No matter; Travis wouldn't have cared if anyone saw him anyway. He'd been down this hallway before, lots of times. He was dressed casually in jeans that were not so new or so old as to attract attention and the old SVU sweatshirt he'd bought way back during orientation week. Except for one little item, he looked like any typical SVU student—which he was. He smiled, although no one would have been able to see it—not through the heavy black ski mask he was wearing.

He twitched his nose slightly to align the eye-holes so he could see where he was going. He knew where Enid's dorm room was pretty much by heart, but he couldn't make even the slightest error today. Everything had to stay perfect.

"Hello?" Her sweet voice came timidly across the line.

"Enid, my sweet. How are you this fine morning? You found the present I left for you, I take it."

She choked back a scream. "You're insane!"

"Grumpy, grumpy. Does this mean you're not a morning person?"

"How do you know my phone number?"

Travis laughed indulgently. "The same way I know where you live. Where you go. What you do. I know everything there is to know about you." He lowered his tone. "I also know that you've been on the phone already this morning. Who could you have been talking to for so long? I was trying to reach you, and it was driving me mad." He pressed the cell phone closer to his ear. The battery was running low, and the static was beginning to bug him. "You haven't been making naughty calls, have you?"

"It's none of your business who I've been talking to. You don't own me."

"Not yet, but you might as well comb your gorgeous curls and dab a little gloss on those luscious lips of yours 'cause I'm coming for you soon."

"Don't ever come here again. Do you hear me?"

"Oh, come on, Enid. Be friendly. I know you like company. Don't you want me to come for a little visit?"

186

"No. Don't come here. If you do, I'll be gone."

"I don't think so, my precious—because I'm here right now."

With a chuckle he flipped closed his cell phone, shoved it into his back pocket, and banged his fist on Enid's door.

Chapter
Twelve

"It's him!" Alexandra shouted. His knock echoed throughout the room. She dropped the phone with a clatter.

Trina's eyes practically bugged out from her pitiful little face. "Did you lock the door?"

Alexandra shook her head. "I thought you did."

Trina made an unintelligible sound and leaped from the bed. She was halfway to the door when the knob began to turn. "The closet!" she squawked, jumping inside.

Terrified, Alexandra dived in right behind her. Just as she slammed the closet door closed she caught a glimpse of a figure in blue jeans and a dark ski mask.

In the darkness she searched for something to secure the door. A belt! With fumbling fingers she grabbed a sturdy leather belt from a hook on the wall and twisted the buckle end around the doorknob. Gasping for air, she struggled to push the empty hook through one of the belt holes. It slipped from her sweaty, shaking hands. As she ducked to retrieve it she could see two shadows moving in the light under the door. Her adrenaline pumping, she grabbed the free end of the belt and pushed the hook through one of the holes.

"You're a genius," Trina whispered.

Alexandra put her hand over Trina's mouth and pushed her back as far from the door as space would allow. She felt as if she were in a clothes-lined tomb. The space was so tiny, there was hardly room for one person to turn around, much less two.

"I think he's looking under the beds," Trina whispered.

"Shhh—," Alexandra said, sticking a finger to her lips. "If we can hear him, he can hear us!"

As footsteps sounded right outside the closet door Trina slid to the floor and covered her head with her hands.

"Get up," Alexandra whispered. "Trina, there's no room in here. . . . This isn't an earthquake drill. Get up."

Using Alexandra's leg as a handgrip, Trina obediently pulled herself to her feet. The two of them silently watched the shadows moving under the door. Waiting.

The doorknob rattled. A knock pounded. It was quickly followed by a hard yank. Alexandra held her breath. The door budged, but just barely.

The shadows moved away from the door. He'd given up! Alexandra wanted to kiss the scuzzy dorm-room carpet, her ratty old sneakers, anything. Then the shadows moved, quickly this time.

Thump! The shadows moved back, then forward. *Thump!*

"He's trying to break in," Alexandra whispered. "Oh, my gosh, he's going to break through the door."

Trina whimpered in response.

"Grab something," Alexandra ordered, feeling around for a possible weapon.

"What do you want to do, stiletto him to death?" Trina whined pitifully. Tears sparkled in her eyes.

Alexandra grabbed a long coat. If she threw it over his head, maybe she'd buy them enough time to escape. But in the tiny confines of the closet there'd be barely enough room to get past him. After she grabbed the coat, she realized something was missing. Two things, actually. The thumping against the closet door . . . and the shadows moving in the light underneath it.

Slowly, cautiously, Alexandra eased her way over to the closet door and pressed her ear against it. Seconds stretched into an eternity.

"I don't hear a thing," she whispered back at Trina.

Trina cowered. "What's he waiting for?" she whimpered.

Me, Alexandra thought.

Trina slumped to the floor. It had been—who knew, five minutes? Ten? Twenty?—since she'd seen or heard anything. Her wobbly legs had given out, refusing to hold her weight. She wasn't just terrified out of her wits anymore. No, now she was feeling awfully darn claustrophobic on top of it. She figured she was going to be stuck in the tiny closet forever, waiting for a psychotic, bloody-earring-wielding maniac to come in and kill her. Maybe the suspense would kill her first.

A raspy noise suddenly echoed around her. It took her a few moments to realize that it was the sound of her own breathing. Trina wondered if the killer could hear it too.

Is that why he's being so quiet? she wondered. *Is he just out there listening to us panic?* She put her hand over her mouth and tried to breathe more quietly, but there didn't seem to be enough air.

I don't want to die in a dorm-room closet, she told herself, warm, wet tears rolling down her cheeks. *I don't want to die anywhere.*

Pushing her hands against the sides of the

closet, she forced herself to her feet and adjusted her baggy pajama bottoms. She'd be ready to make a run for it if she had to.

She looked at Alexandra, who still leaned against the door with that stupid coat in her hands. Then she heard something. She cocked her head to be sure she wasn't imagining it. There it was again.

Someone had called her roommate's name. Alexandra. Not Enid.

"It's Noah," Trina whispered.

"Alex? Where are you?"

Trina lifted her eyebrows. "See, it's Noah. Don't you recognize your own boyfriend's voice?" She reached over to unhook the belt, but Alexandra pushed her hand away.

"Maybe it's a trick! Maybe Travis is holding a knife to Noah—using him to lure us out!"

Trina let out a loud groan and shoved Alexandra out of the way. "Don't be a freak. I'm telling you, it's *Noah*. He probably scared the other guy away!" Before her roommate could stop her, Trina undid the belt and yanked open the door. Noah blinked with surprise as the two of them tumbled out of the closet together.

"See? He's alone," Trina said. "Duh!"

"Oh, Noah, it really *is* you!" Alexandra cried. She flew into his arms.

Noah gave Trina a confused look over Alexandra's

shoulder. "What's going on here?" he mouthed.

"Did you see him?" Trina asked, ignoring his question.

"Who?" Noah asked. "I didn't see anyone. When I got here, your door was standing wide open and no one was around. I wouldn't have come in, but I—"

Trina hurried to the door, slammed it, locked it, and leaned against it.

"Don't lock us in," Alexandra cried, breaking away from Noah's arms. "We don't know for sure that he's gone." Her hand flew to her throat, and she spun around hysterically. "He could still be here . . . hiding under a bed!"

Alexandra was filled with overpowering relief after Noah got down on his hands and knees and peeked under both twin beds.

"Nothing but a few dust bunnies," he announced, climbing to his feet. "And . . . oh . . . Did anyone lose this?" He dangled a purple bra aloft. With a squeal Trina snatched it out of his hand.

How dare he joke around at a time like this! Alexandra thought angrily. *He's not taking this seriously at all. He probably doesn't even believe us.*

"There *was* someone in here, Noah," she insisted. "Are you sure you didn't see anyone?"

"Not a soul."

"Noah, you *had* to. He was here just minutes before you. The doorknob was turning, and the next thing we knew, there *you* were. Ask Trina if you don't believe me."

"I believe you, Alex," Noah said evenly. "But if someone was here, they're gone now."

"Yeah," Trina agreed, stepping between them. "It's a good thing you'd asked him to come over."

Alexandra narrowed her eyes. "I didn't invite him over. In fact, we broke up last Sunday. I asked him not to come over again—ever." She grasped the bedpost to steady herself, then leveled her gaze at Noah. "Just what are you doing here anyway?"

"Um . . . am I missing something?" Noah asked. He made a show of looking around the room. "I'm not mistaken; I just got a hug from you about a minute ago."

"I'm serious," Alexandra said, her voice quavering. "I want you to explain what you're doing here. And don't tell me that you just happened to be in the neighborhood."

"OK." Noah crossed his arms with a swagger. "I just happened to want to see you."

Slowly backing away from him, Alexandra stared at the man she thought she knew—and loved too. The truth was suddenly staring her right in the face, and she didn't want to believe it. But who else was always harping about Enid? Who else knew her phone number, and room number, and her schedule at the hot line? And who'd arrived just in the nick of time to save them—coincidentally right when the killer vanished into thin air?

She remembered something she'd seen when he leaned over to check under the beds. There had been a bulge in the back pocket of his jeans. Was it a phone? Or maybe a ski mask?

"What's in your pocket?" she asked suspiciously.

"What pocket? What are you talking about?"

Alexandra reached around him and yanked the lump from his back pocket. "What's this?"

"It's a phone, Alex. What's it look like?"

"Since when did you start carrying a cellular phone?"

Noah ran his hand through his hair and exhaled loudly. "Since I'm on call at the psychology clinic two days a week. We're working on some pretty intense experiments, and they have to be closely monitored. The phone belongs to the psychology department. See?" He pointed to a "property of" sticker on the back.

Alexandra backed away from Noah slowly. She didn't like the way the veins in Noah's neck were sticking out. He was getting angry. She didn't want to make him mad. She didn't want to turn him into Travis.

"Listen, Alex," he said through clenched teeth. "I don't know what this is about, but I'm worried about you."

Not as much as I'm worried about you, she thought. Never in her worst nightmares would she have imagined Noah capable of killing someone. But Noah had turned into a stranger. And strangers were capable of just about anything.

"What's going through your head, Alex?" Noah asked, frowning with deep concern.

"I—I think you'd better go," she said, her back against the window.

"What's your problem?" he roared. "Are you getting this suspicious about everyone, or is it just me?"

Trina caught his arm. "Noah, one of Alex's sorority sisters has been murdered. You can't blame her for being nervous."

"I'm not upset because she's nervous. I'm upset because she thinks I had something to do with it. You do, don't you?" He stormed toward Alexandra, and she flinched. "You think I'm somehow mixed up with Susan's murder!"

"Of course she doesn't!" Trina insisted.

"Let *her* talk, Trina." Noah stepped closer to Alexandra. She slipped away from him, and he followed her across the room. "Alex, come over here and answer me. Do you honestly believe I killed someone?"

She managed a feeble head shake. It wasn't the least bit convincing.

Noah let out a derisive snort. "You are totally paranoid, you know that?"

Alexandra's shoulders slumped as if she'd just been beaten. "I guess that goes along with all the other personality disorders you've diagnosed for me, Dr. Pearson."

"Yes," Noah deadpanned. "As a matter of fact, it does."

"Maybe I should leave," Trina suggested.

"No! Don't leave me alone with this jerk," Alexandra demanded. She leveled a ferocious gaze at Noah. "So, are there any other psychological aberrations you'd like to add to my diagnosis before you *leave?*"

Noah crossed his arms. "Do you really think for one minute that I had anything to do with your friend Susan's death?"

"Of course she doesn't!" Trina bounced around the room like a yappy little dog. "Tell him you don't, Alex! This is crazy!"

He ignored Trina and concentrated on Alexandra. She didn't say a word, but she didn't have to. She wasn't faking it. She was afraid of him. He could read it in her face. The wide-open eyes, the flared nostrils, the pale sweaty skin, the trembling lips—it was a classic, textbook look of terror. She honestly believed he was capable of murder. He knew she'd been changing for the worse, but he hadn't realized she was quite so far gone.

"You need help, Alexandra," he growled. "You need *serious* psychiatric help."

Her arm flew up. He wasn't sure whether she meant to strike him or push him. He took no chances. He grabbed her arm.

Trina gasped and backed away.

"Alexandra, be still," he commanded. "You're hysterical. You know me. You can't possibly believe I'm capable of murder."

"How do I know?" she cried tearfully. "I never thought you were capable of breaking my arm either, but you're about to!"

He dropped her arm and locked his fingers behind his neck. She was making him crazy. But he couldn't stop himself.

"Admit it, Alex," he said, forcing a gentle note into his voice. "You know I'm no killer. I'm not leaving here until you calm down and convince me you're OK."

She rubbed her wrists. "Yes, yes. You're right," she said shakily. "I am OK now, really. I was just hysterical. We both were. Right, Trina? We got so scared, it made me jump to conclusions. Of course I don't think you could hurt me . . . or anyone." She never took her eyes off his for a moment. The right words were there, but her tone was lacking the least bit of conviction or sincerity.

"That's it!" he shouted bitterly. "I've had it with your problems. I loved you more than you'll ever know, Alex. But evidently that doesn't mean a damn thing to you. You've changed so much, I—I don't even *recognize* you. You're not the woman I fell in love with."

He jerked at the door, his frustration mounting when it didn't open. After fumbling with the lock, he made his escape without a backward glance. He paused only long enough to slam the door with all the fury that was boiling inside him.

Chapter Thirteen

"It's the wrong time of year for Halloween makeup, *Enid*," Alexandra snarled at her reflection. She stuck out her tongue at the ugly face staring back at her.

If only it were a mask, she wished. If only she could wash away the gray, sickly complexion, the puffy, dark-circled eyes, and the tired, droopy lines around her mouth. She tightened the lid on the bottle of ineffective concealer and dropped it back into her cosmetic bag. Why bother? She was fighting a losing battle. What could she expect after only two hours of sleep?

She looked longingly back at her bed. It was still so early. Maybe she'd be better off just crawling back into it and pulling up the covers. But it wouldn't do her any good. She wouldn't be able to *sleep*.

The phone's ring pierced the air. Wincing in pain, Alexandra looked over her shoulder, willing the horrible ringing to stop. It didn't.

Ring . . . ring . . .

She crossed the room but stopped with her hand poised above the phone. *I can't answer,* she thought. *I just can't. It might be him . . . again.*

Ring . . .

"Why won't you just give up?" she whispered hoarsely.

She sank into her chair and pressed her hand to her heart. *He knows I'm here. But I can't let this monster get to me. I have to live my life.*

She jerked the jangling horror up to her ear but said nothing. Just held the phone—waiting.

"Alex? . . . Alexandra, are you there?"

She sighed with relief. It was only Fred. Even *his* grumpy voice was a pleasant surprise. She never thought she'd see the day.

"Yes. I'm here," she said.

"I'm glad I caught you before classes," he said. "I need you to come in to the hot line today."

"Fred, it's Thursday. I'm not scheduled again until next Monday."

"I know that. But sometimes schedules don't work out, do they?"

"Why me? I've worked more hours this past week than any two volunteers put together. Call someone else."

"There's no one else to call. Richard, Vicky, and Cindy have all quit. For absolutely no reason!"

Oh, I can think of a reason, she thought with a wry smile.

"I'm going to run over to the hot line office and open up, but I'm sure not going to stay there all day," Fred rattled on. "I have too many important things to do. I can't sit there all day listening to people bellyache. You've got to help me out."

I can't go to the hot line, Alexandra thought. *It's too dangerous. Something about my working at that place sets Travis off.* But she couldn't explain her fears to Fred. She'd tried once. Her brow creased as she remembered how unsympathetic he'd been. If he didn't care about her feelings, why should she care about his?

"I—I've decided that I'm going to have to cut back on my hours at the hot line, Fred," Alexandra improvised. "Grades come first, you know."

"Well, I'm not surprised that you can't handle the pressure," he replied snottily. "I didn't think the hot line probably was the best job around for an ex-drinker. But I'm really in a bind here. How about this? You work today, and you can cut back next week after we find some new recruits."

She rolled her eyes. What was it going to take? "Actually, Fred," she began, trying a new tack. "The problem is, I'm not feeling well." It wasn't a

202

total lie. She'd never felt so awful in her life.

Fred snorted into the phone. "Who is?" he said. "I have a cold myself, but you don't hear me whining. But if you're sick, you're sick, I guess."

Alexandra relaxed slightly, gratified that he'd bought her excuse. Now she wouldn't have to go to the hot line, where she'd have to die a little bit every single time the phone rang.

"Oh, but Alex . . . ," he added, almost as an afterthought.

"What?"

"If you don't come in today, don't bother coming in anymore at all."

Alexandra couldn't believe her ears. She didn't want to be banned from the hot line forever. It was far too important to her. And if Travis called again . . . well, maybe she had some ammunition to fire back at him now. Maybe she could find out for sure if he was Noah. And maybe, if fortune smiled down upon her, he wouldn't call at all.

"OK," she relented with a huff. "I'll work *one* extra shift. That's all."

"I guess that's better than nothing."

"I'll be there after art class," she said. She was dreading it already.

On Thursday mornings sculpture class was studio time only. As long as they completed their assigned projects, students were free to come and go whenever they liked. Terry was usually nearby in his office in case anyone needed help, but there was no structured lesson or lecture.

Luke stood beside Alexandra's oversized hunk of limestone, anxiously awaiting her reaction. He'd been helping out with—well, *working on,* to be honest—her sculpture over the past two nights.

"Luke, I can't believe how much you've done!" Alexandra cried. "You must have been here all night long." When she smiled, it more than paid for all his effort.

"Well, I needed something to keep me busy last night," he said modestly. "I was . . . well, you know."

"Craving something to drink?"

He nodded. "I called, but you weren't at the hot line. Some crabby guy answered and told me to shape up and join Alcoholics Anonymous."

"Fred." Alexandra rolled her eyes. "I'm sorry. But you know what? Now that we're friends, you could just call me at my dorm when you need to talk."

Friends. The word was music to Luke's ears. "Really? You wouldn't mind?"

"Of course not." She leaned over the table and jotted her number on a scrap of construction paper. "There." She handed it to him. "Call me anytime."

While he carefully folded the scrap of paper

and tucked it into his pocket, Alexandra walked around the memorial stone. She paused, her finger against her chin as if deep in thought. "Hmmm, Luke, correct me if I'm totally off base here, but that face—it sort of looks like . . . me."

Luke scratched his head. "Well, I didn't know what your friend Susan looked like. But you said you wanted the face to look like an angel and . . ." He paused in frustration. Why was it always so hard for him to say what he meant around her? Regathering his courage, he tried again. "When I think of someone beautiful enough to be an angel, I think of you."

Color rushed to Alexandra's pale cheeks. "Wow. That's really sweet, Luke. I wish I *were* that beautiful. Lately, though, I'm afraid I look more like a scarecrow than an angel. This morning I looked in the mirror and saw Enid staring back at me."

"That's funny," Luke said. "You know, I've been thinking about Enid lately."

Alexandra whirled around. Sparks practically flew out of her eyes. "Not you too!" she shouted. A few heads turned.

"Not me what?" Luke asked, blinking in surprise.

"You're not going to start harping about Enid too, are you?"

"S-Sorry," he stammered, wondering why she'd

suddenly turned so defensive. After all, she was the one who'd brought Enid's name into the conversation. "I didn't mean to make you mad. It's just that I've been thinking a lot about changes. I remembered what you said about being Enid in high school. I thought it was great how you were strong enough to turn your life around the way you did. And I was hoping that maybe you could give me some pointers on how to do it."

Alexandra calmed down as quickly as she'd blown up. "Sorry, Luke," she apologized. "I didn't mean to be so touchy. It just seems like everywhere I turn these days, someone is wanting me to be Enid."

"That's not what I meant at all." He pulled off his glasses and laid them on the table. "I guess I didn't express myself very well. I never do, it seems like. But remember in class the other day? When we were talking about making changes and overcoming the past? Well, I've always *talked* about it. And I've always said it was an important thing to do. But the truth is, I've never had much success changing my own life. And I want to. I really, really want to—no, I *have* to—make major changes in my life."

"You make it sound so urgent," she said with a shaky laugh. "But I think you're great the way you are, Luke."

He broke out in a sweat and blushed like a

junior-high kid who had been asked to dance for the first time. There was no way that he could explain to her that this was the very thing he wanted to change. Why did he have to be shy and tongue-tied? So awkward and immature? He wanted to be cool and confident. Sure of himself—especially around girls. Most especially around Alexandra.

"What is it you want to change?" she asked as if she'd read his mind.

"Remember when I first called the hot line?" he said softly. "I blamed my drinking on loneliness. That's always been a problem with me, but my actual problem goes much deeper. It's . . . it's . . . just me. Let's face it, I just have a rotten personality. I'm a big coward. I always hide away with my art or with a bottle . . . always looking for some crutch to get me through the day. I know it's all my own fault. The only way to change my situation is to change myself—from the inside. But it's so hard."

"I know what you mean. My crutch used to be my best friend, Elizabeth Wakefield," Alexandra said. "All through high school I went wherever she wanted to go. I pretended her friends were my friends. Liz always made sure I was included, but we always did what she wanted to do. It was like I'd just handed my life over to her and said, 'Do something with it.' She meant well, and I'm not blaming her. But what she didn't realize was, she wasn't helping me. She was hurting me by holding me back."

"But you changed."

She nodded. "Definitely."

"And I can too."

"Most definitely!" She smiled until she glanced at her watch. Suddenly the smile fell off her face.

"Late for meeting your boyfriend again?"

"No. I'm not even sure I have a boyfriend anymore. It's Fred, the guy who's in charge of the hot line. He's being a real ogre lately about work. He's bullying all the volunteers, then when they quit, he can't figure out why."

"You aren't quitting, are you?"

"No way. The hot line is too important to me." She laid down the polishing cloth she'd been using on the stone. "I didn't really plan to work today, though. I have this statue and the base to finish, and I'm behind in a couple of classes, but Fred doesn't care. He's such a jerk. Can you believe he plans to be a psychologist someday? I feel sorry for his future patients. If they aren't crazy when they come in, they will be after a couple of sessions of his browbeating."

Luke listened sympathetically. He had fully intended to ask her out today, but the time just wasn't right. Anyway, she didn't need someone like him messing up her life. She clearly had enough guy problems already. If only he could think of a way to help her out.

"Don't worry about the statue," he offered. "If you'll wet down that clay for the pedestal, cover it, and get it put away, I'll take care of your tools and clean up here. In fact, if you don't mind, I might stay here and work on the stone a little more. You go on to the hot line."

When Alexandra arrived at the hot line office, Fred was perched on the edge of his seat and tapping his pencil against his desk impatiently. "Well, it's about time!" he snapped.

"Top of the morning to you too, Fred."

"Where have you been?"

"In the art building. I told you I wouldn't be here till after sculpture class."

Fred let out an angry huff. "Since when does art class last three hours?"

"It doesn't. It's a studio class, and it's scheduled for *two* hours," she explained. "But then it took me about fifteen minutes to clean up."

"Why didn't you start cleaning up before the period was over? That would have made a little more sense, don't you think?"

What do you care? she wondered. "No. Actually, I don't." She crossed her arms angrily, totally tired of his bullying attitude. "I have other things to do besides volunteering at the hot line, Fred. Like *taking classes*. And as I mentioned earlier, I wasn't scheduled to come in at all today."

She slung her heavy book bag off her shoulder and let it fall to his desk with a loud thunk. "I told you I would be here, and here I am. If I'm later than you expected, then I'm sorry. But at least I showed up."

"I guess you expect me to feel honored."

"Feel whatever you want," she said, shoving her way past him and settling into the third phone cubicle. "Do you want me to work, or do you plan to stand there giving me a lecture all day?"

He sneered. "My, my, *we're* not in a very good mood today, are we?"

Suddenly the phone rang. For the first time in over a week she was grateful to hear it. "Hello, SVU Substance Abuse Hot Line," she answered quickly.

As a girl began to talk about her problem with diet pills Alexandra smiled at Fred and indicated with a nod and a flick of her wrist that he was free to leave. But Fred didn't. He stood towering over Alexandra's chair, listening to her end of the conversation with a superior smirk on his face.

Alexandra shifted uncomfortably in her chair. "Uh-huh . . . I see. Where did you get the pills after the doctor's prescription ran out? . . . No, you don't have to tell me names. I'm just worried that they might not be the right drug for you— not if a doctor didn't prescribe them. . . ."

As Alexandra listened she could practically feel Fred's breath on her neck.

Go away, she pleaded silently. She could hardly think what to say to the caller with him so close. "I—I have some numbers here of support groups you could call if you'd like."

Alexandra rose from her chair, forcing Fred to back off slightly. She began to shuffle through the items on the cluttered bulletin board, looking for the brochure on eating disorders and diet support groups. Her hands were shaking so badly, she shouldn't have been surprised when she accidently pulled out the wrong tack and papers dumped down all over the floor like an avalanche. But even as self-conscious as she was feeling, Alexandra was able to retrieve and read off the numbers of the support groups, and she still managed to do a good job of calming the caller down.

When she hung up, Fred was still there. He leaned over her, one hand on her desk, the other on the wall. "Alex, can we talk?"

What now? she wondered. There wasn't anything left for him to gripe about. Definitely not the call she'd just fielded. She handled that call strictly by the book. And she did a darn good job of it, especially considering the fact that Fred was hanging over her head like a storm cloud the whole time.

She looked up at his scraggly goatee and sighed loudly. "Sure, Fred. Let's talk," she said, giving in.

He leaned so close, she could smell the cinnamon gum he was chewing. "I was wondering if you'd like to have dinner?"

"What?"

"Dinner. You know, food in a restaurant. With me." Fred moved his arms around in some sort of moronic sign language to accompany every choppy word. "Do you think we can go out sometime?"

The invitation was so unexpected, she couldn't help herself. She burst out laughing.

Fred turned beet red and stumbled backward.

"I'm sorry," she said, waving her hands and fighting for self-control. "I didn't mean to laugh. It's just that when you said that . . . that was the absolute last thing I expected you to say. I didn't mean—"

"Forget it!" he snarled. "Forget I ever asked. I don't know why I did anyway. I must have been feeling sorry for you. I wouldn't really want to go out with anyone so callous and heartless. Just forget I ever suggested such a stupid thing."

Alexandra felt as if she'd been slapped in the face. "OK, fine. It's forgotten."

Fred ran his hand over his bristly red hair. "You're really rude, you know that? I guess it must give you a real rush to put guys down.

Believe me, I know your type. Homely in high school, you blossom late in life and then give guys hell—revenge for all the years you weren't Miss Popularity."

Alexandra gasped. "I'm not like that at all!"

"Oh yes, you are, Alex . . . or Enid . . . or whatever the heck you're calling yourself today."

"And you're an ogre, Fred. A big, overbearing, bullying ogre! I don't know why *anyone* would ever go out with you."

"You think I'm an *ogre?* How poetic—not to mention perceptive," he said sarcastically. "No wonder you have so much trouble on the phones. You're so wrapped up in yourself that you can't see anyone else's problems. The hot line needs volunteers with empathy and sensitivity." He narrowed his beady eyes at her. "Even a rookie with the most rudimentary knowledge of psychology should be able to see beyond a person's protective mask. I know that I may come off a little gruff at times, but—"

"A little gruff! Is that what you call it? Then I'd hate to see you if you *tried* being a hateful bully." Alexandra snatched up the papers from the floor and slammed them down into a semistraight stack on her desk. "I stand by my original statement, *Dr.* Freud—I mean *Fred*. You are an absolute ogre, and I wouldn't go out with you if you were the last man on campus."

Although she didn't think Fred's posture could get any straighter, it seemed to as he stuck out his chin, turned, and stalked out.

"Good riddance," she muttered after hearing the outer door slam. She dropped her head onto her folded arms as if she were exhausted. She was tired, yes. But she was far too worked up to sit still.

I'm not awful on the phones! she thought indignantly. *He's just jealous of my success rate, the big jerk.* She'd been working at the hot line a lot longer than he, and she'd never had any complaints—except from him. Take Luke, for instance. He couldn't have been more complimentary about how she'd helped him. Sensitive, caring, and perceptive. That was who Alexandra Rollins was.

The ringing phone jangled into her thoughts. She reached over and picked it up without thinking.

Chapter
Fourteen

"Hello, Enid, sweetheart," Travis crooned. He cupped his hand around the phone so the people walking toward Parker Hall couldn't hear him. "How are you today? Are you wearing your new earrings?"

"You're crazy."

"Crazy about you."

"No. You are seriously out of your mind!"

Travis let her words roll off his back. He was in too good a mood to let her cute little tantrum annoy him. Everything was working out just the way he wanted. Life was looking up.

"Travis," Enid said, her voice suddenly adopting Alexandra's official, insincere, robotic tone. "You have to stop this. You say you care about me. Well, if you really do, I want you to listen to me. You have to turn yourself in, for your own good."

Travis laughed abruptly. "I'm just starting to live. I'm not about to give myself up now."

"You have to. You need help. . . . I mean . . . I want you to get the help you deserve."

Travis left the sidewalk and ducked around the side of the dorm. "Now *you're* the one who's sounding crazy," he hissed. He slipped behind some bushes and leaned against the side of the building. "If I turn myself in, they'll lock me up." He switched the cellular phone to his other ear and peeked out of his hiding place to make sure he couldn't be seen. "Everything would be spoiled. If I was locked away somewhere, our love could never be."

He thought he heard her sigh.

"But don't you worry, Enid. I'll never let that happen. I'm here for you—always. I will never let you down."

"I don't want you to be here for me. I want you to leave me alone."

Travis laughed again. "You love me, Enid. You may not realize it yet, but you *do* love me."

"No! I don't. Get that through your thick skull. I could never love you."

"You will. As soon as you see the real me, you'll know that I'm the perfect man for you. When you see behind the facade, you'll realize what kind of guy I really am. I'm caring and considerate. I'll always be sensitive to your needs.

I'm not an *ogre* like that jerk Fred. . . ."

"Fred!" Enid gasped into the phone.

The slam of her hanging up echoed around in Travis's brain. He stared at the phone in seething silence. Why did she do that? Why did she hang up on him again? He shrugged out of his backpack, unzipped it, and tucked the phone inside. Then he pulled out his knife and a sharpening stone.

I didn't even get to tell her my new plan to show her how much I love her, he lamented.

"Oh, well," he mumbled with a sigh. Slowly he ran the stone down the gleaming blade of his knife. Then faster. There in his shadowy hiding place, the steady scraping sound seemed to calm him. "I'll just tell her about it afterward."

"Travis is really Fred. . . . Fred is Travis. . . . Oh—whatever!" Alexandra muttered. Her heart was pounding in terror as she ran into the outer office. She'd called Fred an ogre right to his face and not fifteen minutes later he was on the phone, repeating that very phrase right back to her. It could hardly be a coincidence. "I've got to call the police before Fred kills someone else!"

Alexandra slammed her fist on the bare surface of Fred's desk in frustration. Of course he'd lock up the only phone in the place with an outside line. If he was a murderer, he wouldn't want her to call for help, would he?

Probably the phone is bugged anyway, she thought. *Probably this whole place is. I've got to get out of here!*

She thought of using the phone upstairs in the psychology lounge, but if she called 911 or even if she called the police station directly, she'd still have to go through all the levels of red tape. She'd waste precious minutes retelling her story umpteen times, just the way she'd had to do the day before. Her best bet was to call Detective Kaydon's private number—but it was lying beside the phone on her desk back at Parker Hall.

Parker Hall it is, Alexandra thought. She grabbed her book bag and flew out the door. She didn't stop to work out all the details in her head. She only knew that she had to get to the police before Fred—or Travis—or whatever he was calling himself hurt someone else.

If people spoke to her as she dashed across the quad, she didn't notice. Her mind was focused on one thing only.

Oh, please, she prayed, *please let me convince someone that I'm right—someone who'll have the power to stop Fred in time!*

Trina paused in front of the door of 409 Parker Hall, her key in hand, only to find it not only unlocked but ajar. She wasn't at all surprised that the housing office hadn't bothered to change their lock yet. What did a little matter of life and death mean to them? Still, this turn of events was unsettling, to say the least.

"Alex," she called, pushing the door cautiously inward. "Alex, are you home?"

Carefully Trina inched her way forward. Just as she'd stepped over the threshold someone crashed into her from behind. Trina screamed and grabbed at the doorknob to keep from falling.

"Trina! It's just me."

"What's going on?" Trina asked, stumbling to one side as Alexandra plowed past her.

"I've got to get to the phone," Alexandra said breathlessly.

Trina sighed, thankful that her scare was only a false alarm. "What's your rush?" she asked as she turned to shut and lock the door. "And why hasn't the housing—"

"Where's that number I wrote down for Detective Kaydon?" Alexandra asked.

Trina heard the sound of shuffling papers and then the sound of the phone receiver being lifted. She was reaching toward the closet to hang up her jacket when an earsplitting scream shattered her senses. She spun around to find Alexandra standing in front of her desk, pointing at the floor.

Trina's blood froze as she followed the line of Alexandra's pointing finger. There, sticking out from under her bed, right where the bright floral dust ruffle met the institutional green carpet, lay a fish-belly white hand, palm up. Its fingers curled slightly.

As badly as Trina wanted to scream, she didn't. She couldn't. The best she could do was gag. Hand over her mouth, she backed against the door, hoping her stomach would settle before the inevitable happened.

Alexandra dropped the phone with a clatter, jumped over the hand, and grabbed Trina in a bear hug. "I walked right past it and didn't even see it," she sobbed. "I just had to get to the phone—I can't believe I didn't step on it."

They hugged tighter. Someone was whimpering. Trina wasn't sure whether it was Alexandra or herself. She couldn't take her eyes off the hand to find out. She half expected it to reach out and grab one of them, but it didn't move.

Reaching over blindly, Trina placed a hand over Alexandra's mouth, and the whimpering became muffled. She began to gulp to calm her own breathing down.

"It's a fake!" Trina shouted, recovering control of her voice. "A Halloween prop. They sell every creepy body part imaginable in all those party stores. Someone is just trying to scare us, that's all."

Alexandra pulled Trina's hand from her mouth. "Well, they're doing a really good job of it!" She swallowed loudly. "You really don't think it's real?"

Trina shook her head. "Of course it isn't. It's

just a horrible mean prank, like the earrings."

"Then *you* look under the bed. I can't."

"Nuh-uh. I can't either."

"Then we'll do it together," Alexandra suggested, tugging Trina by the arm. "I'll lift the covers, and you look."

At first Trina nodded agreement, but then she dug in her heels. "Wait," she said so suddenly, it made Alexandra jump. She grabbed her umbrella and held it over her shoulder like a club. "OK. Now I'm ready."

With agonizing slowness Alexandra crept toward the hand. Almost in slow motion she caught the edge of the comforter between her thumb and first finger and daintily lifted. Trina crouched down and peered beneath the bed.

What she saw there caused her to lose her balance. She landed smack down with a thud. The hand wasn't fake. It was a real hand . . . sticking out of a real shirt . . . worn by a real guy. He was lying on his back, but his face was turned sideways. He was staring right at her. Blood had seeped from beneath him and was oozing out from under the bed in a gooey dark puddle.

Still sitting, Trina scooted away—too terrified to make a sound. She didn't even think she was breathing anymore.

"What is it?" Alexandra asked, stubbornly refusing to look for herself.

"It's a guy," she gasped. "I don't recognize him. . . . Red hair . . . pale skin . . . a cheesy goatee . . . a bloody shirt." Every couple of words she had to pause and force herself to breathe. "He's . . . he's . . ."

"Fred?" Alexandra dropped to her knees and bent her head to look. She screamed and turned as pale as the corpse.

"You know him?"

"My new boss at the hot line. Remember? I told you what a horror he was."

"But . . . how? . . . Why?"

Alexandra's head began to shake. "D-Do you think we should check his pulse?"

"*You* check his pulse. It's *your* boss, and he's under *your* bed." Trina shrank back. "But I wouldn't touch him if I were you."

Alexandra gingerly lifted the pale hand and pressed her fingers to its wrist. "Nothing," she said, letting the hand fall back to the floor.

Trina wasn't surprised. Fred certainly looked dead to her.

"I thought it was Fred," Alexandra mumbled. "That's why I was trying to get to the phone. I can't believe I was wrong. He asked me out and we had a fight and I called him an ogre and he left . . . and I . . . and then I got a call from the killer and—"

"Alex, get a breath. You're not making sense."

222

"I thought Fred was the killer."

Trina began to giggle. Nothing was the least bit funny, but she couldn't stop herself. She was so terrified, it was as if all her emotions wanted to come out at once. "Boy, were you wrong," she said.

Alexandra glared at her. "I was going to call Detective Kaydon and tell him that Fred was the killer. Now I don't know what to tell him."

"You could start by telling him you have a dead body under your bed."

"Trina! We've got to get out of here. If Fred's not the killer, then that means Travis is still out there. I—I just talked to him a little while ago. And he—he's been here and left . . . *this* just in the time since Fred left the hot line. He's probably still here in the dorm somewhere."

Trina's giggles turned to tears. "Call the police!" she screamed. "If you don't, then I will. They'll have to believe you now. They can't very well call this a fraternity prank!"

While Alexandra was talking to Detective Kaydon, Trina moved over to the window and hunkered there, as far away from the gruesome sight as she could, but it was no use. Her eyes kept going back to the hand and to the ugly black pool that was seeping out further and further from under the bed. She was going to have nightmares every night for the rest of her life, she just knew it.

Unable to take the ghastly sight a moment longer, Trina took the tip of her umbrella and gingerly scooted the hand under the bed. With a shiver she dropped the comforter back in place like a final curtain.

"You probably shouldn't have touched that," Alexandra whispered, her hand over the receiver.

Trina just shrugged and shook her head. She'd simply have to admit to the police what she'd done. They'd understand . . . she hoped.

"They'll be right over," Alexandra said, relaying the message from the phone to Trina. "Detective Kaydon said not to touch anything . . . else," she added pointedly. "Not to go anywhere. And not to let anyone else in till they get here."

"They don't have to tell me to stay put. I don't think my wobbly legs would carry me as far as the elevator." Trina dragged her desk chair over to the window and plopped heavily into it. She pushed open the blinds and turned her back to the room. "I'll watch for the cops."

"Yes, sir. We will be careful," Alexandra said into the phone. "*Please* hurry."

Trina heard the clack of the receiver being replaced. But no sooner had Alexandra hung up than the phone rang.

They both jumped and screamed.

"I can't answer it." Alexandra backed away from the phone.

"You have to."

"I so do not have to!" Alexandra wailed.

"Yes, you do," Trina murmured, shock setting in at last. "It's probably the police calling back."

She heard Alexandra pick up the phone. "Hello?" she asked tentatively. When she screamed, Trina put her head in her hands and sobbed.

Travis couldn't help but laugh as Enid shrieked and babbled incoherently. She was so cute when she was terrified.

"So, I take it you found my next gift," he said. "That's good. Do you see now how much I love you? I took care of that horrible Fred for you, just as I'll take care of anyone who makes my Enid unhappy. You can count on me, my love."

"No. No," she sobbed.

"Yes, yes," he replied with a chuckle. "There will be no more Freds in my Enid's life. Only Travis. I am all you need forever and ever. And soon we'll be together."

"No!"

"Is that all you can say, my love?" He sat back and polished the blade of his knife. The ogre's blood was gone now, washed away forever. "Well, that'll change. I know Alexandra still has some reasons to stick around, but soon—thanks to me—they'll all be gone and you, Enid, will be free to be yourself. Then we can enjoy the eternal

225

splendor of our love. Just you and me. Nothing will come between us."

He shook his head with tolerant compassion as she began mumbling nonsense into the phone. He wasn't angry with her. She was simply confused and frightened, but she would understand—he'd see to it that she would. Very, very soon.

"Good-bye, love," he whispered, breaking off the connection. The resistance she felt wasn't her fault. She would come around as soon as he got rid of her other so-called friends.

He polished the blade of his knife until it gleamed. How he loved to polish his knife, especially after a fresh kill. With a robust laugh he began to dance around his room impatiently. He couldn't help it. He was already excited about the next gift he had chosen for Enid.

The moment Noah's fist rapped against the door to Alexandra's dorm room, a pandemonium of screams broke out from inside.

"Alexandra!" he yelled, throwing his weight against the door. He bounced off, knocking off his cap and nearly jarring his shoulder out of place. Undaunted, he picked up his cap, stumbled back to the door, and beat on it with the flat of his hand. "Alex," he bellowed, "what's going on in there? Let me in. It's me, Noah."

"I know who it is. Now go away!"

He considered ramming against the door again—trying to break through to her—but he could tell from the sound of her voice that she was leaning right against it. "Are you OK in there?"

"As if you care!"

"Alex, this is crazy. Of course I care. I'm here, aren't I?"

"Yes, you are," Alexandra whimpered. "The question is, what are you doing here?"

"Don't start that again. I miss you. I want to talk to you. Why else would I be here pounding on your door?"

"You must think I'm really stupid if you believe I'd fall for that line."

Noah pounded on the door again. "Alex, *this* is stupid. I don't want to stand here talking through this door."

"Then go away!"

"I won't. Open this door right now and let me in."

"I've already called the police. They'll be here any second."

Police? Noah's stomach lurched, and his knees started to give way. He leaned heavily against the door. "Listen to me, Alex," he pleaded. "This is important. Let me in and I'll tell you the real reason I'm here. It's too bizarre to discuss . . ." He trailed off. "OK. I didn't want to do this, but I have no choice." With a sigh, he took the set of keys to room 409, Parker Hall, from his pocket and began trying them in the locks.

"What are you doing?" Alexandra screeched.

"I found your keys, Alex," Noah explained. "They were right outside—"

Alexandra let out a bloodcurdling scream.

"What's the big deal?" Noah cried. "I thought you'd be happy I—"

"They're here!" Trina shouted. "I just saw two cars drive up!" Suddenly the door was yanked open and Alexandra and Trina burst into the hallway as if they'd been shot from a cannon. Noah had to jump back to keep from being bowled over. The set of dorm keys dangled limply in his hand.

He stared in amazement at Alexandra's wide, terrified eyes in a face so pale, her freckles stood out like ink dots. Trina was so close to her, the two of them appeared to be joined at the hip. But in reality they were joined at the hands—hands so tightly clutched together, their knuckles were white.

"Alexandra, listen to me!" Noah hollered. "I didn't say this earlier because I didn't want to scare you."

"*You* took my keys!" Alexandra screamed. "It was you all along!"

"What?" Noah blinked in confusion. "No! I just found them over by the fire stairs. Listen, the *real* reason I came over here was because I was worried about you. . . ."

The door to room 407 opened and Cheri Beinveni stuck her head into the hall. "What's with all the noise? I've gotten about fifty calls telling me to turn down my TV, and it ain't even on."

"Cheri!" Alexandra screeched hysterically. "Don't come out here. Get back in your room! And stay there till it's safe."

With a look of horror and surprise, Cheri jumped back inside and slammed her door.

Noah laid his hand gently on Alexandra's shoulder, but she and Trina sidled away. "Listen, about why I came over here," he began again. "I got a weird creepy phone call that scared me—"

Alexandra cut him off. "You *made* a creepy phone call, you mean. You have gone too far this time, Noah Pearson. I don't know what's going through your mind, but don't try sneaking away. The police are on their way up here right now."

"There's a—a body in there," Trina stammered.

"You don't have to tell him anything, Trina," Alexandra broke in. "He knows there's a body in our room. He's the one who put it there!"

"You've really lost it this time, Alex," Noah grumbled. He craned his neck to see into the room.

"No, *you've* lost it." Alexandra jabbed a finger in his face. "*You're* crazy. Certifiable. I don't know what's happened to you, but anyone who could do the things you've done has to be totally insane!"

"Alex, I don't know anything about a body—"

229

"Save it for the cops." Alexandra peeled her fingers free of Trina's grasp and hugged her arms around herself. "Don't pretend you don't know what I'm talking about. I know it was you, Noah. You're the one who's always harping about Enid. You're the only one it could be. What do you want? Why didn't you scurry away like you did after killing Susan? Did you stick around to get more of my friends? Have you come back for Trina?"

With a terrified howl Trina took off down the hallway. Two uniformed policemen had just stepped out of the elevators.

"Trina? What in the world would I want with Trina? Have you gone completely out of your mind? I just came over here because—"

"Here come the police. Let's see if they believe your explanations, *Travis!*"

Travis? But Noah didn't have time for another word. Trina and her cops from the elevator had arrived. Noah gasped in shock as the beefy hand of a very large policeman closed down on his shoulder like a vise. As he was pushed roughly against the wall he saw two other policemen burst from the stairwell with guns drawn.

A virtual troop of police officers had taken over the floor. One was stationed at the stairwell door, another at the elevator, and Alexandra had no idea how many were going in and out of her room. She, Trina, Cheri, and Noah had been moved out of the way—down to the TV lounge at the end of the hall.

On one side of the narrow room Trina and Cheri sat on a tattered couch, whispering. On the opposite side Noah sat, swelled up like a bullfrog, his wrist handcuffed to the leg of a table. And in between Alexandra fidgeted on a chrome-and-vinyl monstrosity of a chair.

Detective Bart Kaydon was standing in front of Alexandra, jotting down notes on a clipboard.

"Ask him!" Alexandra ordered, hysterically wagging her finger in Noah's direction. "I've told you five times everything I know about Fred. Ask Noah why he stuffed Fred's body under my bed!"

"Miss Rollins, calm down. I've got to get a statement from everyone, and there are certain questions I need to ask. If I repeat myself, just try to be patient." Detective Kaydon's voice was calm and fatherly—just like his appearance. He seemed to be in his early forties, with salt-and-pepper hair, a serious five o'clock shadow, and the bluest eyes she'd ever seen. He was trim and neatly dressed. And except for the badge hanging on a string around his neck and the gun tucked into the small of his back, she would never have guessed he was a policeman.

231

Alexandra shifted uncomfortably. "Why won't anybody believe me? I'm telling you—just like I told those other two policemen when they first got here. He's your man."

"I didn't do anything," Noah protested. "Sir, you've got to believe me."

Alexandra snorted. "Yeah, right! Ask him where he was earlier this afternoon—about four."

"Miss Rollins, let me run this interrogation, OK?"

"I was in my dorm room," Noah said, ignoring Detective Kaydon and answering Alexandra directly. "I didn't leave there until I got this crazy call. Some little wimpy voice warned me that Alexandra was in trouble. So I hightailed it straight over here. The next thing I knew you guys had me cuffed to a chair." He rattled his handcuffs noisily.

"Noah, I told you—"

"I know. I know. For my own good . . . safety of others . . . thanks for my cooperation and all that. I heard the routine from you and King Kong over there. But I didn't *do* anything."

"OK. Let's take this one step at a time," Detective Kaydon said, tapping his pencil against his clipboard. "How long have Miss Rollins's keys been in your possession?"

"I told you, I just found them today," Noah replied impatiently. "About two minutes before I knocked on Alex's door. They were on the floor by the fire stairs."

"Liar!" Alexandra cried.

"Miss Rollins." Detective Kaydon shot a warning look in her direction. "Now, Mr. Pearson, can your roommate verify that you were in your room all afternoon?"

"No. I was there alone—studying."

Alexandra rolled her eyes. "Right! Poor Noah. *All* alone, *all* day with nobody around who can swear to your whereabouts. That's the sorriest excuse I've ever heard. Well, *I* can vouch for you. I know *exactly* where you were. You were on the phone with me, and then you stalked Fred and killed him. And then you brought him here to me like some deranged cat leaving a mouse on the doorstep."

"I didn't! I don't even know this Fred guy!"

"And what about when Susan Zercher was killed?" Alexandra said, turning back to Detective Kaydon. "Ask him where he was last Thursday morning."

Noah wanted to cross his arms, but he was hindered by the handcuffs. He yanked at them in annoyance. "How am I supposed to remember what I was doing a whole week ago?"

"Yeah, right. Imagine that. No alibi that day either!" Alexandra gripped the arm of her chair. "He did it, Detective Kaydon. He killed both of them. There's no one else it could be!"

"Thursday. Oh yeah. I remember now. I didn't go to classes that day. I—uh . . . slept in."

"Hangover?" Detective Kaydon asked, managing to get a word in.

"No, nothing like that."

"How convenient!" Alexandra sneered. "It's amazing that you'd suddenly just remember that."

"Alex, I remember because it was the morning after we had that fight. You know, on the way back from Pasquale's. I was so upset afterward, I couldn't sleep. I finally crashed around four the next morning and didn't wake till nearly noon."

Detective Kaydon sighed and flipped to another paper on his clipboard. "Am I to understand that you two are dating?"

"Not anymore!" Alexandra said.

The detective ran a hand through his hair. He started to say something but was interrupted when a female officer poked her head into the lounge.

"Detective," she began, "we've questioned nearly everyone on this floor. Several heard screams, but they apparently didn't investigate or even think much of it. They all assumed it was Miss Beinveni's TV." Everyone turned and looked at Cheri. "It seems she watches a lot of slasher movies."

"All right. Thanks, Officer Brown." Detective Kaydon rubbed his chin thoughtfully and looked from Alexandra to Noah and back to Alexandra. Pursing his lips thoughtfully, he addressed Officer Brown. "Since you're finished here, I think maybe you ought to transport Mr. Pearson down to the station."

"But—," Noah protested.

"Noah, go with this nice lady," the detective ordered. "Don't make this hard on yourself. When you get to the station, you can make some calls, answer some questions, and we'll get this all straightened out."

Noah slumped against his chair until Officer Brown recuffed both hands, behind his back this time. He shuffled away at her side without a backward glance. Alexandra felt suddenly relieved but at the same time strangely sad.

Detective Kaydon turned back to Alexandra. "All right now. Let's see if we can't finish this up. Correct me if I'm wrong. You and Noah Pearson are not boyfriend and girlfriend now, but you *were* up until this past week, when you had a fight?"

"Yes," Alexandra agreed. "More evidence that he's the killer, right?"

He shook his head. "No, just the opposite. The fact that you two were a couple and have been fighting might simply mean that you're angrily jumping to conclusions about him. Or maybe even trying to get him into trouble as a way of revenge."

"I'd never—"

"I'm not saying you would. But stranger things have happened, and believe me, it's the kind of thing a defense lawyer would push to the fullest."

"Noah did it. I know he did it," Alexandra muttered as Detective Kaydon busily jotted in his notebook. She crossed her arms over her chest and chewed at her bottom lip while he knelt in front of Trina and Cheri.

"What about you, Miss Slezniak? Do you think Noah is our killer?"

"No," she said quietly. "Noah is really quiet and smart and . . ." Alexandra whirled to face her and glared. "Well, m-maybe . . . I don't know!"

Reading the annoyance in Detective Kaydon's eyes, Alexandra clamped her mouth shut and moved over to the doorway while he got statements from Trina and Cheri.

Things seemed to be quieter on the floor, but there was still a lot of activity. As she watched, a man and a woman from the coroner's office wheeled a gurney out of her room and down the hall to the elevators. She felt nauseous, thinking that Fred was zipped inside the dark plastic bag on top of the gurney.

A hand gripped her arm, startling her. "You don't really think Noah could do such a thing, do you?" Trina whispered.

"Yes!" she snapped. But seeing Trina wince, she realized her nerves were making her strike out at everyone. "Trina, you don't know what he's been like the past couple of weeks. Noah has totally changed. He's been so full of rage lately. It's like the littlest thing sets him off. It scares me." She paused, watching as the gurney was wheeled into an elevator. "Yes, I think he did it."

"Really?" Trina asked. "I mean, come on, we're talking about Noah here. He loves you . . . but not to the point of killing for you, you know?"

Alexandra looked up at the light fixture. Two dead moths rested inside the concave shade. She bit her lip, trying to hold back a sudden gush of tears. "I'm telling you, he's gone crazy! Why doesn't anyone believe me?" Suddenly Alexandra could hold it back no longer. She burst into loud, noisy sobs. Trina patted and cooed, but it didn't help much.

I love Noah. I really do, she told herself. *But how could this be happening? Can someone change that quickly? How could he lose his mind so suddenly? Why didn't I see it coming? There must have been warning signs. People don't just go insane overnight, do they?*

When he finished questioning Cheri, Detective Kaydon joined Alexandra and Trina and walked them down the hallway, where an officer was slapping tape on their door.

"I'm afraid you and Trina are going to have to find another place to spend the night," Detective Kaydon said. "It might be a bit of an inconvenience, but it'll be better all around. Just in case this nut isn't long gone."

"But you've arrested Noah," Alexandra protested.

"No, we haven't. We've merely taken him to the station for questioning. If we find further evidence, we can arrest him, but right now—there's not much to go on. I don't want to upset you, Alexandra," he said, patting her arm gently. "But we won't be able to keep him long."

"H-How long?"

Detective Kaydon shrugged. "He'll probably be back on the street by eleven, midnight at the latest." He nodded to the officer who'd taped up their door. Then he turned his attention back to Trina and Alexandra. "Do you think you can find a place? I could call someone from—"

"No, we can stay at my sorority house," Alexandra said, pulling herself together. "They have extra guest rooms."

"You still have my number if you need me."

Alexandra nodded, but didn't trust her voice to answer.

"OK, then," he said. "Since everything's taken care of here, I'd better get back down to the station."

Right, she thought. *Everything's taken care of. By midnight Noah will be out of custody . . . and then what?*

Chapter
Fifteen

She is so beautiful, Luke thought as he stood outside the door of the sculpture studio, watching Alexandra chip away at the block of stone. *So ambitious . . . and brave.* He admired, and even envied, the courage it must have taken for her to tackle something she'd never tried before. Her memorial was quite an undertaking for a beginner—for anyone. No one could have imagined that she'd have been able to accomplish so much in such a short time. Even without his help she'd done an impressive job. There was no doubt in his mind that she had a lot of artistic talent, even if it did need a bit of developing.

"Hard at it, I see," he said.

Alexandra jumped. "Oh, Luke, it's you. You scared me!"

"Sorry." He pulled off his jacket and draped it

over a nearby stool. "I guess you weren't expecting anyone else to come in here so late."

"What time is it?" She looked at her watch. "Oh, my gosh! It's past midnight. I had no idea."

"Well, I didn't mean to freak you out." Luke retrieved his bust from the shelf and brought it over to his worktable. "I was having one of those nights, you know. . . ."

"Oh, don't worry about it," Alexandra said with a sympathetic smile. "I've been jumping at every little noise. Just a little while ago I thought I heard someone in the . . . Oh, never mind. I'm just edgy."

"That's understandable," Luke said. He wiped his hands on his jeans. "Is it true what I heard today? That somebody found a body in your dorm? I've heard about fifteen different stories, but—"

She set down her hammer and chisel. "Oh, Luke. It was awful. Remember my telling you about Fred?"

"Your boss at the hot line."

"Right. Well, he was killed, and his body was left under my bed." She shuddered. "That's kind of why I'm here. To get away from it all, you know?"

"You don't have to talk about it," he said, sensing that he'd opened a subject she wanted to forget. "But I have been worried about you. Do

241

you know if they caught the guy that did it?"

Alexandra sighed sadly. She stood there chewing her bottom lip for so long, Luke was beginning to think that she hadn't heard his question. "They had a suspect, but I think they might let him go. No evidence, I guess."

"Let him go!" Luke cried. "You mean the killer could still be roaming around and you came over here by yourself?" He pressed both hands to his head and frowned worriedly. "You shouldn't be wandering around campus alone. And you definitely shouldn't be in this art building late at night with no one around. Aren't you scared?"

"A little. But I didn't have much choice. Have you forgotten that our projects are due Monday?"

"No." Luke set his materials out on the table and pushed his bust over closer to where Alexandra was working. "I still have a little to do on mine too. But I can't believe you'd want to be here all alone with a crazy murderer on the loose. I worry about you."

"I'm not alone. You know how this place is. There's always some hard-core art student sneaking in here to finish up a project. See, you're here now, aren't you?"

Luke smiled. "Yes, that's true. But—"

"Besides," Alexandra continued in a more serious tone. "I refuse to let this nut totally ruin my life. I have to keep going." She sighed. "He's already taken so much from me. With Fred gone, the hot line's been closed. I can't face my dorm room. None of my sorority sisters will even *walk* through the TV lounge at Theta house." She looked up at him with tears glistening in her eyes. She looked as if there was a lot more she wanted to say but couldn't. "Anyway, I'm not going to let him take my art away from me too—or my freedom."

"I think you're very brave," Luke said quietly. "I really admire that. I'd have crawled into a bottle by now."

"No, you wouldn't have," she assured him. "You don't give yourself enough credit. I can tell you have a lot of courage."

"Well, that's why I'm here—to get away from temptation." Luke's face burned, and he turned away. He put on his glasses, bent over his sculpture, and began to work the paper core out of the clay shell. He cleared his throat and held up the bust. "I think I need to take just a little clay out of the inside. Clay is sort of funny—making it too thick actually weakens the piece."

"Yeah, nothing's worse than a thick head," Alexandra teased.

Luke smiled. "How's the memorial statue coming?" he asked, hoping to turn the conversation away from himself.

"Pretty good, I guess. I'm finished with the

pedestal. The inscription turned out really great, but I'm still a little worried about the shape. I hope I didn't make the top too narrow." She ducked her head and pointed. "It's there under the table if you want to look at it. And as soon as I finish this edge of the second wing, I'll be done with this main stone. If you're going to be around for a while, maybe you'll help me set it on top of the base later."

"I'm not going anywhere," he said. "And I'd be happy to help. Just as soon as I fix the damage here and pop this masterpiece into the kiln, I'm all yours." He blushed and rolled his eyes. "I mean, I—I'll be free to help you," he amended.

She smiled. "Great. Because there's no way I could do it myself. That thing must weigh a ton."

"Tell me about it," he said, bending over with his hands at the small of his back. "I'm the one who loaded it into your car, remember?"

She pushed back her hair and gazed at him, her green eyes shining. "Seriously—I appreciate all your help, Luke. Not just helping me get it to the car, but all the work you've done. The face is so great. It has turned out just—"

Luke held up his hand, silencing her. It wasn't just her praise that was making him feel uneasy. He was sure he heard something out in the hall. "Wait here."

"Wha-What is it?"

Luke went to the studio door and looked out. "Nothing," he said as he returned to his work space. "I guess I'm getting jumpy too. Alexandra, I don't mean to be nosy, but why . . . why didn't your boyfriend walk over here with you? I mean—"

Alexandra seemed to draw into a shell. "I don't have a boyfriend anymore. We . . . broke up." She whacked her hand instead of the chisel and cursed under her breath.

"Are you OK?"

"Fine. I'm fine, just clumsy."

They worked in silence for several minutes. Luke kept sneaking glances in her direction. He knew he was going to have to ask soon, or he'd never get his courage up again. He wiped the clay off his fingers, climbed off his stool, and started toward Alexandra. Almost as an afterthought he paused, pulled off his glasses, and plunked them atop his self-portrait bust. His heart pounding, he cracked his knuckles, stretched, and finally moved over to where Alexandra was bent over her memorial.

"Alexandra," he began, "I—I . . . well, maybe it's too soon, and if it is, I'll understand, but . . . well . . ." He pressed his lips together and scowled. Asking Alexandra out was harder than turning down a free drink.

She straightened up, laid the chisel and hammer atop the limestone, and turned to face him.

"What is it, Luke? Is something wrong? You look so serious."

Her eyes were so understanding, so calm and sympathetic—so green. How he adored her! *It's now or never, Luke,* he decided.

Taking a deep breath, he plunged bravely ahead. "Alexandra, I guess you've already figured this out, but I need to say it. I really, really like you. I was hoping . . ."

Her gaze never wavered. A sweet smile played upon her lips. Was he going to make it?

"I was hoping maybe you'd go out with me sometime." There. He'd said it. And she hadn't run away, hadn't laughed in his face. She just sat there, smiling.

"I'd like that, Luke." She put her hand on his arm. It was a good thing she held on. Her hand was an anchor holding him to the floor. Without it he'd float away with happiness.

"Maybe tonight?" he whispered. "When we get through here? We could take a walk, or go get something to eat."

She tossed back her beautiful copper waves. "I don't have any other plans, and a walk in the moonlight sounds great. Actually, I was hoping you'd ask. I've . . . been thinking about you a lot lately. I like you too."

Luke opened his mouth and snapped it shut. Just in the nick of time he'd stopped himself from blurting that he loved her. *Take it slow,* he reminded himself. He couldn't afford to scare her off now, not before she even had a chance to get to know him. "Wow, I—that's . . . really, really great news," he blathered.

Alexandra drew closer to him. So close, he realized that if they stood body to body, his chin would barely touch the top of her head. He looked down at her, hoping he didn't look strange to her from where he stood.

She turned her face up toward his. "I'm glad you think so, Luke," she whispered. She placed a hand on each of his arms, drawing him closer to her.

Luke leaned down, and like magic, Alexandra's lips touched his. He couldn't believe it was happening. It was just a brief, friendly kiss, but he felt as if he'd died and gone to heaven. Suddenly nothing mattered anymore. He had no problems, no fears. Nothing but a happiness he'd never felt before. Could she really like someone like him? Really?

He pulled her to him and kissed her again— gently, worshipfully, tenderly. He savored the sweetness of her lips.

"Wow," she whispered as they broke apart. "That walk in the moonlight is sounding better and better."

"Give me five minutes." He rushed back over

to his project. "No, make it three." He held up three fingers. "Or one!" He ran back over to her side. "Are we finished here now? I'm ready to go if you are," he asked with a grin.

She laughed. "Actually, I *am* done. If you'll help set this stone on top of the base, then I'll be ready to go."

Luke yanked up the sleeves of his gray sweatshirt and pretended to spit in his hands.

Alexandra shook her head good-naturedly. "I've never seen you in a mood like this, Luke," she said. "What's gotten into you?"

"You," he said, meaning every inch of it. "Now let's get the hard labor over with so we can have some fun."

"Sounds like a plan to me."

Luke grunted and strained until he and Alexandra had wrestled the heavy stone into place.

She wrinkled her brow. "I'm still worried about its stability. You don't think I've made the clay pedestal too narrow, do you? Do you think it'll hold the weight of that stone?"

"Sure, once it sets overnight, it'll be as strong as one solid piece. How you get this thing out of here, however—*that* could be a problem."

"Well, I don't have to think about that now, right?" Alexandra swept up her rock dust and tossed it in the trash can. "OK. I'm ready for that walk now."

"Ohhh, I can't—not yet," Luke lamented. "I really need to finish up my project." He felt a pain shoot through his head. He pinched the bridge of his nose and winced.

"What's wrong?"

"I'm getting a headache," he said. "I think it's the solvent fumes from the painting studio next door." He rubbed the back of his tense neck. "Are you thirsty? I think maybe I'd feel better if I just . . . had something to drink. Would you mind getting us a couple of sodas from the machine down the hall? Maybe I can get my head back together in the meantime."

"Which head? Your real one or your clay one?"

"Both, I hope," he said with a laugh. He fished in his pocket and brought out a handful of change, which he handed to Alexandra. Headache or no headache, he'd never been so deliriously happy in his whole life.

Alexandra smiled to herself as she dropped quarters into the soda machine. Maybe this night wouldn't turn out so badly after all. Her sculpture had turned out even better than she'd hoped— thanks to Luke. And what's more, now she wasn't alone. Imagine finding someone to care about in the midst of tragedy. It didn't make it all right, but it sure made things feel better. Like there was new life to be found, new boundaries to explore.

"Love . . . love is strange," Alexandra sang to herself.

Love. She couldn't say that, not yet. Who knew? Maybe she wouldn't be able to say that at all. Only time would tell.

Although she couldn't deny her attraction to Luke, she was still feeling mighty confused. She didn't want to rush things with him, not as long as Noah was still in the picture—upsetting her, confusing her. Maybe even lurking in the background or outside the studio . . . watching, waiting for her.

As she made her selection she realized that Noah really was out of the picture romantically—this time for good. Alexandra laughed derisively at herself. How long did it take for her to come to that conclusion? There Noah was in her dorm—the only thing missing was the blood on his hands. And here she was, getting nostalgic at a stupid soda machine, still carrying a tiny torch for him!

"You get mixed up with the wrong guys, Rollins," she murmured to herself. "It's time to move on."

Why not to Luke? He liked her, and he was certainly cute. Maybe a little shy, but his kiss— mmm, nothing shy about that. She smiled, remembering the gentle touch of his lips against hers.

But what about Noah! her conscience nagged.

A canned soda clunked into the dispenser at the bottom of the machine, and Alexandra robotically fed it a few more coins.

Noah was probably out of custody now. The hairs rose on the back of her neck; she could practically feel his presence. She wanted to call Trina at Theta house, but she'd probably lay another Noah-is-innocent trip on her. Well, maybe Noah was free; maybe—*hopefully*—he wasn't. But at least she hadn't heard from him or seen him—*yet*. And hopefully she wouldn't if she kept hanging out at the studio. There was no way Noah would come looking for her at the studio, right?

Alexandra pecked at the choice button three or four times in frustration after the machine took her money. It wouldn't give her another soda. She tried another selection but still had no luck.

She dug into her own pockets until she found enough change and poked it into the machine. The second can dropped into the slot with a clunk.

Just as Alexandra was reaching for the soda, the pay phone on the other side of the soda machine rang. Alexandra jumped and stared at it. It remained silent. She was just imagining things. That was all.

Another ring pierced the air. Louder than the last. Alexandra winced.

Ignore it, she told herself. But she knew she couldn't. It could be Trina checking up on her or giving her some news on Noah's whereabouts. Or maybe it was someone looking for Luke. She approached the phone warily. There was one voice she didn't want to hear.

Nervously she picked up the receiver. "H-Hello?"

"Hello, Enid, my love."

She gasped. Her heart leaped to her throat, practically choking her.

"May I say you look ravishingly beautiful tonight? You're practically glowing—like a young woman in love. Having fun with Luke?"

"H-How do you know about Luke?" she stammered. *"Where are you?"*

"Right behind you."

Enid's delicious scream rang clear and true in the air. Fear; it was so cleansing. When Enid's knees buckled, Travis grabbed Enid in his arms. "Hello, my love."

Now we're getting somewhere, he thought, watching her innocent eyes grow wide. As the blood drained from her face Alexandra disappeared, leaving only Enid to shine through.

How beautiful she is when she's terrified! he mused. *The magical power of terror brings out the little girl in her, the scared little girl whose name will always be Enid. I love her.*

252

Holding her tightly, he buried his face in her hair and breathed deeply, taking in the smell of her perfume, the applelike scent of her hair. His heart pounded with excitement.

He had waited so long to have her in his arms. Now here she was at last; her closeness was driving him over the edge. He pressed his lips to her neck.

Her fist broke free and struck his shoulder. He winced. Quickly he recaptured her arm and held her more tightly for her own good. Her struggles were futile. Travis wasn't scared or even worried that Enid would run away. Only that Enid would vanish and Alexandra would reappear. Struggling would bring Alexandra back— Travis knew that. And Alexandra didn't love him, he knew. But it didn't matter. Because after tonight Alexandra would be no more. Even if she decided to reappear.

"Luke! Help me!" Enid screamed as Travis yanked her roughly backward and dragged her down the hall. She kicked and fought, but it was no use; Travis was too strong for his Enid. Her fingernails swiped his ski mask once, yanking it slightly off center. His sunglasses, held tight under his mask, bumped painfully against the bridge of his nose.

Travis paused and rubbed his face against his shoulder to put his mask and sunglasses back in place. He didn't loosen his hold on her for a second. It felt too good to hold her, kicking and screaming, knowing that Alexandra would be dead forever before the sun came up.

"Luke!" she screamed again. "Please help!" Again she broke free and clawed toward his face.

Puffing hard, Travis caught her hand and twisted her arm behind her. She cried out in pain.

Alexandra's pain, he told himself. *She's weakening. I must stay strong for Enid. I must help Enid through this trial. I must . . .*

Stiffening, she stopped struggling and leaned toward him, as if she was trying to stare into his eyes. She was trying to see through his sunglass lenses, Travis could tell. Impossible. But he liked how hard she tried and the way she did it most of all. She brought her face close, so close, to his. He could feel her breath on his lips. Delicious.

"Noah?" she asked. "Noah, is that you? Don't do this to me."

Travis shook his head and laughed.

She cocked her head to one side and peered at him like a little bird. He knew she couldn't see a thing. She was only guessing.

"You're . . . oh, my G—Luke—"

"No," Travis replied with a grunt. She was still not cooperating. As he dragged her down the hall her feet made an awful noise, scraping and scooting along the floor. Good thing he wouldn't have to listen to it much longer.

With a final surge of effort he pulled her into the

art room and kicked the door shut. "There's your precious Luke!" he snarled, twisting her around.

A canvas-covered lump lay in the corner. A lump that was once a body. On the floor beside it Luke's wire-rimmed glasses lay twisted and broken.

"No!"

"Sweet, naive, helpful Luke," Travis sneered. "Gone and hopefully forgotten. Dead as he deserves to be. He really wasn't the right guy for you, you know. You need a *real* man. . . ."

Alexandra stared at the hidden form that had only a few minutes earlier been a warm, living, breathing, *kissing* young man. She slumped backward, landing herself deeper into Travis's grasp.

"Oh, how touching," Travis drawled in his deep, gruff voice. "You're brokenhearted. Don't tell me you'll miss that wimp."

Alexandra's anger flared. She started to scream.

Clamping a hand tightly over her mouth, Travis dragged her farther into the room. "Shut up!" he yelled into her ear. "No one is around to hear you. No one! I'm warning you. Be quiet. Or else . . ." He ran a finger up and down her torso. Alexandra nearly vomited. "Well, you don't *want* to know what I'll do if you scream." He laughed and adjusted his grip on her head. It was so tight, she could hardly breathe.

Roughly Travis tipped her off balance and

shoved her toward a tall metal stool—the very stool Luke had been sitting on only moments before. Holding her arms behind her with one hand, he reached across the wide, scarred art table for a ball of twine. Alexandra struggled to break free of his grasp—and to keep the angry, confused, grieving tears from falling. It was useless. The tears spilled, leaving wet drops on his black sweatshirt.

"Awww, poor thing," Travis taunted. "Would you like to join your boyfriend right now? Huh?"

Suddenly Travis waved a knife in front of her face. She stopped struggling, stopped crying, her spine ice-cold with fear. She didn't even see where the knife came from. It just practically appeared out of thin air.

"Now be still," Travis urged. "No more fighting. I don't want to use this . . . on you."

She froze. *Is this what he used on Luke?* she wondered. Her gaze darted from the glistening steel back to the shadowy corner. Tears filled her eyes. *And on Fred? And Susan too?*

Is this what he'll use on me?

Yes.

She was next. She knew it.

Travis shoved her down on the stool so hard, her teeth jarred. Then he tossed the knife to the table and roughly tied her hands behind her. She flinched as he tightened the rope with a final yank. She hardly moved as he carelessly tied her legs to

256

the stool. She was his prisoner. Travis's prisoner. She was trapped.

This can't be Noah, she thought urgently. *He would never threaten me with a knife. We were in love. . . . Surely I would recognize his voice, his eyes—something about him!*

But who else could it be?

"There, that ought to hold you for a while." Travis backed away and admired his handiwork. He grabbed a handful of clay and leaned into her face. "Now keep quiet or I'll stuff your mouth full of this."

Alexandra kept quiet.

"Are you ready for your next surprise?" Travis asked teasingly. He dropped the lump of clay and wiped his gloved hands on his black sweatpants.

She didn't respond, didn't even move. He picked up the knife and tapped her leg with it. She could feel the sharp point prick her thigh through the thick material of her jeans.

"Enid? Yoo-hoo, are you in there? Do you hear me? I asked you if you're ready for your next surprise, sweetheart."

"Y-Yes," she stammered.

He tossed the knife onto the table behind her and scurried away like a rat.

When he'd disappeared through the door, Alexandra craned her neck around toward the table. *If there was only some way I could get to that knife,*

257

she thought. She rocked backward, but it only made the stool teeter precariously. With a gasp she grabbed the edge of the metal seat as the stool settled back on all four legs with a thud. It was no use. If she fell over, she'd have no way to break her fall. And Travis would probably be so mad—

"Ouch," she muttered. A rough place on the underside of the stool had scraped her fingers. Tears sprang to her eyes. She didn't know how badly she'd been cut, but it sure stung.

Muffled noises from the next room suddenly took her mind off her fingers. She could hear what sounded like a squeaking chair and then the rattle of rollers on the old hardwood floors.

She whipped her head around and watched in horror as Travis wheeled something into the room. He had some poor fool trussed to a desk chair like a fly in a spiderweb. It looked like a guy, but she couldn't be sure—not with the large brown grocery bag over the person's head.

Travis stopped the chair right in front of her, so close that if her ankles hadn't been tied to the stool, she could have reached out and touched it with her foot.

"Ta-da!" Travis sang. With a flourish he yanked the sack away.

The tousled dark blond hair, the deep-set brown eyes—

"Noah!" she gasped.

Travis ripped the tape off Noah's mouth. "Alex," he croaked weakly.

"This creep was spying on you earlier tonight," Travis said. "But I got to him just in time. He didn't see you and Luke carrying on." He leaned down in Noah's face. "You didn't see the big kiss, did you, boyfriend?"

Alexandra winced. She'd been wrong—so wrong. How could she have suspected Noah all this time? Now he was being ravaged by a psychotic killer—a killer whose identity was now a complete mystery. And it was all her fault.

"You wouldn't have liked it—Luke and Enid kissing," Travis continued. "Trust me. It would have made you want . . . to kill someone. No, it's a good thing you were off taking a little nap." Travis laughed like a banshee. He turned back to Alexandra and laid his hands on her knees. "Fooled you, didn't I?"

"Who are you?" Alexandra screamed.

"Travis, love."

"Travis who?"

"Travis who loves Enid. That's all you need to know."

Alexandra started to cry.

"Stop it!" he warned. "I can't stand that noise!"

Alexandra sniffed. Unable to wipe away her tears, they rolled messily down her cheeks. She looked down at Noah, and catching his eye, she mouthed the most inadequate phrase she'd ever uttered:

"*I'm sorry.*"

Noah nodded grimly. *You* should *be sorry,* he thought. *If you hadn't kept insisting that I was the killer, I might have been able to protect you.*

Heaven only knew how much he'd tried. Ever since the police had released him, he'd been trying to track Alexandra down. Frantic about her safety, he'd headed straight to Theta house. He found Trina, but Alexandra had her so terrified of him, she wouldn't talk to him at first. It had taken him nearly twenty minutes to worm Alexandra's whereabouts out of her.

The very idea that Alexandra would come to the art building all alone at night with a killer on the loose not only scared him, it infuriated him. How could she be so foolish? He'd rushed to the art building like a madman. After locating her and seeing that she was OK, he'd calmed down. He'd just settled into a perfect hiding place in the painting studio when someone whacked him over the head with a piece of pottery.

Noah could still see the pottery shards and dust on his jacket. His head still throbbed. And that cold sensation on the back of his head—was that blood? He couldn't tell.

But now was not the time to dwell on the past

or on his condition. His eyes were still open, his mind still awake. He had to keep his head clear and figure out a way to get them out of this mess.

Suddenly his chair moved again. Noah watched the madman in the ski mask warily as he rolled him several feet away from Alexandra and then stood between them, hands on his hips, glancing back and forth from one to the other.

"All righty now," the guy said at last. "Are you both comfy? Good. 'Cause we're going to play a little game." He reached across the table and picked up a nasty knife.

Alexandra gasped, but the guy never looked back at her. He just continued to stare at Noah. And Noah didn't dare take his eyes off him.

"Quiz bowl time," the ski-masked creep announced. "You look like a pretty smart guy, Noah. I'm going to ask you *one* question. If you answer wrong, it'll prove you don't love my Enid."

"And?"

Travis touched the point of the knife to the hollow at the base of Noah's throat. "And then I'll have to kill you." The guy seemed to like the thought. "I'll simply have to remove you from Enid's life forever so she'll be free to love me— only me. You see, I plan to have her all to myself."

"But what if I answer correctly?" Noah asked, straining his head back as far away from the knife as his bonds would allow.

The demented, ski-masked creep pulled the knife away and made a choking, laughing sound. "Not likely," he pronounced.

"But I *do* love her," Noah said, catching the raw emotion in Alexandra's eyes for the briefest of moments. "It could happen. What if I get the answer right?"

Travis seemed to ponder the possibility. "Well, then I guess I'd have to let you go."

"And turn yourself in," Alexandra added.

Travis spun around and glared at Alexandra. Raising the knife over his head, he stepped toward her.

"Fair enough!" Noah shouted, drawing Travis's attention away from Alexandra. "Then it's a deal. If I answer correctly, you'll let me go!"

Noah gazed at Alexandra. Her eyes seemed to be pleading with him. Her expression softened suddenly, as if to say that she loved him and trusted him. He felt his heart skip a beat. How wonderful it was to see that loving glow return to her face after such a long absence. Suddenly he was filled with renewed strength and confidence.

"Go ahead," he dared the masked maniac. "Ask your question."

Alexandra's wrists were burning and raw from straining against the rope. Her cut fingers were still hurting, and her shoulders were throbbing from the awkward position of her arms. But none of her aches was nearly as awful as the pain in her stomach as she watched Travis wave the knife so close to Noah's face.

I've got to help him, she thought frantically. *If I could just get . . .*

The twine around her wrists snagged on the underside of the seat. Aggravated, she yanked it . . . *loose!*

Holding her breath, she surreptitiously moved her hands against the twine. Yes, it was definitely looser. Perhaps she had cut through a strand or two. It made sense. If the stool could cut her fingers, then why not her bonds?

Alexandra's heart pounded excitedly. It could work. After all, she wasn't tied with real rope, just the art department's cheap rough twine. She could break it. She had to!

Ignoring the pain, Alexandra slumped slightly and crept her fingers along the underside of the stool until she relocated the sharp piece. Leaning back and twisting her body uncomfortably, she began savagely sawing her wrists against it—never taking her eyes from Travis and the flashing blade of his knife.

Once again Travis leaned dangerously close to Noah. "OK, smart boy. Here's your question. Let's pretend Enid has a big test tomorrow," he said. "But what if she's also been invited to a raging party? A major sorority bash—one that all the most

263

important people are expected to attend. What does she do? Stay home and study, or go to the party?" Travis rocked back on his heels. Even though Alexandra couldn't see through the ski mask, she could just picture his smug grin. But she couldn't imagine a face horrible enough to attach to it.

Noah squinted in concentration.

Travis kicked his chair. "Hurry up! If you really love her as much as you say you do, the answer should be easy."

Noah pursed his lips. "Is it *her* sorority or any sorority?"

Alexandra stifled a gasp as Travis's knife hand visibly tensed. "Any sorority, you *dope*. Just a party. What does it matter?"

She squeezed her eyes shut and tried sending an ESP message to Noah: *Shut up.*

"That's easy," Noah said, almost sounding somehow . . . cheerful?

Travis leaned forward, anticipating Noah's answer.

"She'd go to the party for a while. Then she'd come home and study like crazy at the last minute."

Alexandra sighed with relief. *Noah* does *know me!* she thought, letting her hands go limp. Now Travis would have to let them go.

Travis's reply came as suddenly and harshly as a slap in the face.

"Wrong!"

Chapter Sixteen

"What?" Noah's eyes widened, and his mouth went totally dry. "How can I be *wrong?*" He squirmed furiously against his bonds. "Who do you think you are? You don't know Alexandra better than me. You don't—"

Travis held the knife up for him to see.

Noah's heart and lungs kicked into overdrive as the madman stood inches from his face. Travis ran his finger along the blade of that knife, leaving a thin trail of his own blood. Noah forced himself to look away from the shining blade before his fear paralyzed him.

He glanced at Alexandra, who was frantically rubbing her wrists against something at the back of her stool. He couldn't panic. His survival and Alexandra's might depend on it. And he couldn't let anything happen to Alexandra.

Noah closed his eyes, held his breath, and channeled his fear into anger. "Hey, man, we had an agreement," he lashed out.

"You said that if I answered correctly, you'd let me go. My answer was one hundred percent right. I know Alexandra. And that's exactly what she'd do. Ask her if you don't believe me." His words hung in the air, vibrating with much more bravado than Noah actually felt.

Travis leaned in so close, Noah could smell the sweaty, wet wool of his ski mask. "I didn't ask you what *Alexandra* would do. You weren't listening to me, *boyfriend*. I asked what *Enid* would do." Travis cleared his throat. "Who cares about Alexandra?" he shouted. "Alexandra isn't even real. She only exists in Enid's imagination." Travis took a deep breath. "Don't you get it? I'm talking about Enid. And *I* know Enid. If she was left on her own, she'd stay home and study like a good girl. Sorority parties mean nothing to her."

"She's not *Enid*," Noah insisted. "Her name is Alexandra."

Alexandra gave Noah a look of gratitude that almost broke his heart.

"Alexandra?" Travis asked, a spiteful laugh piercing the air. "Not anymore!" With one hand he grabbed a handful of Noah's hair and yanked back his head. With the other he raised the bloody knife high into the air.

266

Suddenly the ropes that held Alexandra's wrists snapped apart. Her heart hammered against her rib cage as she untangled the twine and shook her tingling hands to get feeling back into them. Quickly she yanked loose the flimsy cords holding her ankles.

"Travis!" she yelled.

Travis turned away from Noah—just long enough. She jumped off the stool, which crashed to the floor right at Travis's feet. Before he had a chance to recover, she plowed into his shoulder, spinning him to one side. With a howl he tripped over the leg of the stool and fell.

"I'll get help!" Alexandra shouted, running for the door. She'd just hit the hallway when she heard Noah scream.

I can't leave him, she realized, skidding to a halt. If she left, Noah would be dead before anyone heard her screams.

Alexandra turned and rushed back into the room. Her eyes widened at the sight of Noah. Travis's knife was pressed against his throat. Deep. She was almost sure he was cutting—

"Travis, let him go!" Alexandra demanded. "Don't you dare hurt Noah, you coward! You're making a big mistake."

Travis hardly glanced in her direction.

He told me that he hates screaming, Alexandra

scolded herself. *It makes him nervous. And I don't want to make him nervous.* She clenched and unclenched her fists. *What can I say? What can I do?*

"Travis," she began again, her voice less angry. "Don't hurt Noah. Please," she begged. "I'll do anything you want. I'll stay here with you. Just let him go. Noah never hurt you."

"No, but he hurt *you.*" He stomped his feet impatiently on the ground. "Come on, Enid, I wanna hurt him back!"

Alexandra stifled a gasp. Travis suddenly sounded like an overgrown, pouting kid! Her hopes sank as she realized there was no way of reaching Travis—none. But suddenly she found inspiration. Her heart pounding and her fingers crossed, she took a deep breath before she began.

"Listen to me, Travis, sweetheart," she said in a soft, cooing voice. "You don't have to do this. You've already proved your love for me. You gave me Susan . . . and Fred. Who else would have gone to so much trouble for little old me?" She stepped closer. "I believe you now. Just like you said I would. I see the real you. I see it all clearly now. No one has ever loved me the way you do."

When Travis's hand wavered slightly, she knew she was on the right track. She took another deep breath and fought to keep her voice soft, almost singsongy. "You want Enid, and she's right here. All you have to do is reach out for her. You told me . . . I'd know when the time is right. Well, I know—it's now. You can . . . you can show me your love now."

Travis slowly lowered the knife. Alexandra knew she'd said exactly what he wanted to hear.

Noah's eyes were wide—his expression horrified. She hoped that he understood what she was trying to do.

Travis rubbed his face mask frantically. "You're not Enid," he griped. "Too much . . ." He continued wiping where his eyes and lips must have been under the mask and glasses.

Makeup? Alexandra quirked an eyebrow. She could hardly recall putting on any makeup, and certainly she wouldn't have bothered on an awful day such as this one. Still, to appease him, she made a show of wiping her face with her sleeve. "There," she said in a small, almost childlike voice. "All gone?"

Travis nodded—and jabbed his knife blade back into the flesh of Noah's neck. "No!" she cried involuntarily. She winced, sure she'd just made a big mistake—but not sure why.

"See, you're not Enid," Travis complained. He rubbed the knife blade along Noah's neck as if it were a sharpening stone. He wasn't breaking the flesh, but Alexandra knew he could at any moment. "You're protecting Alexandra's boyfriend. Bad. Not what my Enid would do."

Alexandra stood frozen in place, dumbfounded. *What does he want me to do?* she wondered, her mind racing. *What should I say?*

She looked into Noah's brown eyes. They were pleading, desperate. And dark too; very dark. He nodded slightly as if he were trying to tell her that whatever she said about him right now, he would understand.

I have to reject Noah, she realized. But how could she now, when she'd just finally realized how much he meant to her—how much she loved him? She felt physically unable to say anything against him. She knew she had to, but—

Noah's eyes widened. More urgently this time. Alexandra looked at his neck. Travis's blade was leaving a long, red welt there. Soon he would draw blood.

"Travis, you know I don't love Noah," she said with a light laugh. Noah closed his eyes and, she hoped, his ears; she didn't want him to hear or see any more of this sick scene. "I hate Noah. I love *you*, Travis. Enid loves you."

It sickened her to say those words. More sickening still was the almost obscene way Travis's sunken chest seemed to puff out at the words; his spine straightened, and his face, still invisible under the ski mask and glasses, seemed to pull back in a revolting, pleasure-filled leer. He let out a long, slow *aaahhh*. But the knife never left Noah's neck.

"Enid, my love," Travis purred.

"Yes?" Alexandra asked, growing more and more disgusted with each second. How much longer would she have to pretend to be Enid? She never wanted to go back. . . . Would she be stuck there forever?

Travis took a long, deep breath. "That . . . was . . . *not . . . good . . . enough!*" he shrieked. "Noah means nothing to you, Enid. He hurt you. He tried to kill you—"

"No!" she insisted. "He never—"

"So you have to hurt him back." Travis waved his knife in the air. "You have to kill him too. Come on, Enid. Help me kill him!"

Alexandra took a tentative step forward. Noah's eyes were wild with fear, so she tried to calm him with a brief I'm-in-control gaze. It didn't work. Tears welled up in Noah's eyes, and his face was whiter than alabaster. Suddenly she had the perfect plan—or so she thought. She just didn't know if Travis would buy it.

"I can't kill anyone, Travis," she declared softly.

"What?"

"Your Enid doesn't kill. And neither should you."

"But he deserves to die. That slut Alexandra is gone forever. Now there's only you, Enid, you and me," Travis raved. "And there's no place for Noah in our lives."

"B-But Noah . . ." She trailed off and looked at the ceiling, stalling for a moment. "Um, Noah has a place in the world, Travis. And I care about the world."

Noah's face relaxed slightly, but Travis's blade swiftly regained its place over Noah's jugular. Both men's bodies shook, worrying her even more. One tiny slip and Noah would be gone forever. She had to think fast.

"But . . . Noah isn't part of *our* world," Alexandra insisted. "You should let him go, Travis. He'll stay away from us. Won't you, Noah?"

"Yes," Noah croaked out.

Travis firmly grasped the back of Noah's neck and brought his knife up, blade pointed down, ready to plunge it deep. "There's only one way to make sure—"

"No!" Alexandra cried. "Travis, stop. Listen to me. Listen to Enid. There's no reason to kill Noah. He doesn't matter. He was Alexandra's friend, and Alexandra is gone now. Only Enid is here now—to love you." She held out her arms to him and hoped he didn't notice how hard they were shaking. "Oh, Travis, I—I love you so much," she said, trying to keep from retching. "Only you. Come to me. Put the knife down and come be with Enid—forever."

Like a child taking his first tottering steps,

Travis stepped toward her, his arms outstretched to meet hers. She jumped when he uttered a strangled cry, but as the knife clattered to the floor she realized it was a sob. Travis was crying.

Travis thought his heart would burst from happiness. He'd never heard such lovely words in all his life—at least not directed toward him. Only someone as forgotten and trampled on as Enid could ever understand. Only this poor little wren could ever love someone as worthless as himself.

Enid's smile glowed at him like a beacon as he rushed toward her. Or he tried to rush, but his feet felt as if they were mired in clay. The faster he tried to move, the slower he seemed to go. *Hurry,* he told himself. *She's there, your angel. Waiting for you. Enid, completely yours at last. You've finally destroyed that horrible, snobby Alexandra mask, that sham, that sorority freak—and now the two of you—the two lost souls—can be joined as one.*

His ski mask was soggy with his tears, and his face was starting to itch from the clingy wet wool. But soon it wouldn't matter. He'd remove his mask, just as he'd removed hers. And they would be together—forever.

Like a runner reaching out for that ribbon at the finish line, he held out his arms for their long awaited embrace and stumbled across the last few feet between him and Enid.

No. What's happening? he thought as her welcoming smile suddenly turned into a snarl. Without warning, an animal-like cry escaped from her bared teeth. He had no time to react before her fist came up in a slow motion arc that connected with his nose with such ferocity and force that it sent him reeling.

I'll kill her, he raged as he stumbled backward into Alexandra's sculpture—that huge, ugly monument to a manipulative wench who deserved to die. *I'll—*

But his thoughts were interrupted by a loud crack. The shattering of clay. The base of the sculpture broke, and the memorial toppled. Travis screamed as the heavy block of limestone came crashing down onto him, smashing him to the floor. Despite the searing, crushing pain in his chest he managed a sobbing breath. "Enid," he whispered. "My Enid . . ."

And then everything went black.

Noah gaped in shock as the dust settled. It was almost too much for his brain to process. He stared at the psychopath, pinned to the floor by a huge gray boulder. He looked like a bizarre turtle with his shell on upside down. He could tell the guy wasn't going anywhere. He and Alexandra were safe, he thought. But at the same time he could still feel the knife being pressed to his throat. He didn't think the sensation would ever go away.   •

"Noah, are you all right?" Alexandra asked. Her fingers tenderly touched his neck. "You're bleeding." She ran over and grabbed the knife from the floor and began to hack at the tape and ropes that held him to that detestable chair. As soon as she had one of his hands free he began to help her.

Freed at last, Noah jumped up on wobbly legs and wrapped Alexandra in a giant hug. He couldn't believe she was in his arms—safe. They were both safe.

"No time for that now," she said, cutting her eyes over to the guy beneath the fallen statue. "I have . . . I have to know who he is."

Reluctantly Noah let her slip from his arms, but he wasn't about to let her go near the lunatic alone. As she ran toward Travis he was close behind. Alexandra stood over Travis. She seemed to hesitate.

"Here. I'll do it." Noah reached down and yanked off the ski mask to reveal a skinny, flushed, ordinary-looking face. A complete stranger. Harmless, a little weak looking. Not the kind of face he was expecting at all. "I've never seen him before," he said, tossing the ski mask to the floor. "Do you know him?"

"It's Luke," Alexandra whispered. She knelt

down beside him and brushed the guy's sweaty hair back from his forehead. "He's . . . he's just a guy from my sculpture class." Her voice broke, and she bowed her head to hide her tears.

Noah had questions, lots of them, but suddenly he noticed the guy's eyelashes fluttering. "He's regaining consciousness," he squawked. He grabbed Alexandra and tried pulling her away, but she resisted. He gave up but left his arm in front of her protectively, like an adult keeping a child from crossing a busy street.

Noah jumped as the guy's eyes popped open. With his free hand Noah felt around on the floor for a broken piece of the memorial—something big enough to club the guy with, just in case he came up with some final superhuman burst of strength like the bad guy always did in the movies. But Travis, or Luke, or whatever his name was, didn't rise up. Except for his eyes, which were focused entirely on Alexandra, he didn't move at all.

Noah held his breath. He dreaded hearing that horrible voice again. If he said "boyfriend" in that creepy mocking tone one more time, Noah swore he would clobber him. His hand tightened around the broken hunk of clay.

But when the guy spoke, his voice sounded completely different than it had a moment ago. If Noah hadn't seen the rock fall—hadn't recognized the same black sweat suit—if he hadn't pulled the mask off the guy himself, he'd have thought a switch had been made. Instead of sounding deep, raspy, and angry, the guy sounded quiet, peaceful—even timid.

"Alexandra," the guy whispered. "I'm so sorry. I broke your angel statue. It was so beautiful."

Alexandra strained forward against Noah's arm—but Noah didn't move the arm away.

"It's OK, Luke," she said quietly. "We can fix it."

His eyelashes fluttered. "Alexandra," he said thickly. "I would never have hurt you." He winced in pain. His fingers twitched, but his hand never lifted from the floor. "I'm glad Travis is gone. I tried to change . . . tried . . . to deny him for so long. He'll never torment me again. . . ."

He took a deep breath that sounded like someone blowing air into a crinkled paper bag. "Oh, Alexandra," he murmured as he exhaled. And then he closed his eyes and was completely still.

"I think he's dead," Noah said.

After Noah had left to call the police, Alexandra reached down once again. She touched Luke's cheeks—they were still pink, as if he were blushing even in death. Despite all the evidence lying around them—the stone, the ski mask, the knife over by the chair—she found it hard to believe that Luke could be a killer. He'd seemed so nice, so gentle. But maybe it wasn't him, not really. Maybe his Travis personality was so scary to him that he'd blocked it out.

Tears streamed down her face as she turned away. Had Luke even known the terrible things he'd done? Killing Susan . . . killing Fred, and . . . *and who else?* She scrambled to her feet and looked at the canvas-covered form in the corner. Who was Travis's final victim? If it wasn't Luke as he claimed, then who? Taking a deep breath, she hurried across the studio. Something crunched beneath her feet; Luke's glasses. Not stopping to pick them up, she continued to the corner where one last horror waited. Names and faces of her friends and acquaintances whirled in her mind. *Don't let it be anybody I know,* she pleaded. Whipping back the canvas, she gasped. There, amid a pile of wadded newspapers, lay Luke's self-portrait bust. Though colorless, the likeness of the pale gray clay was nearly perfect. Luke's gentle eyes, his delicate cheekbones, even his dimples— all perfectly re-created. A perfect replica of Luke's head lay in the corner with a chisel stuck right in the center of his forehead, splitting the head almost in half.

Travis had been telling the truth. Travis *had* killed Luke.

"The police are on their way," Noah announced, coming back into the room.

Alexandra wiped away her tears, but she was

278

too ashamed to turn and face Noah. She had been so awful to him—arguing with him, breaking up with him, accusing him of being a killer. Because of her he'd spent most of the night in jail. Because of her he'd . . . nearly been killed himself!

Although her tears for Luke were spent, fresh ones started to fall for Noah. They'd been so awful to each other. How would they ever repair the damage they'd done? Had she lost him forever?

Alexandra felt a hand on her shoulder. She spun around to face Noah. He had tears in his eyes too. "Oh, Noah, I'm so sorry," she cried, wrapping her arms around him. "I've been so stupid. Can you ever forgive me?"

"Shhh—," he whispered against her cheek. "You don't have to say—"

"I know you love Enid," she interrupted. "I'd be her for you if there was any way I could, but I just can't be her anymore. I still have to grow and change and be who I think I should be. And even if I don't always know *exactly* who that person is, I do know that I love you with all my heart."

"What more could I ask for?"

"But Enid . . ."

"I don't love Enid," Noah whispered against her neck as he pulled her closer into his arms. "Well, maybe I do . . ."

Alexandra squirmed in an effort to pull away, but Noah held her tight. "Let me finish. I was going to say that if I do love her, it's only because she's a part of you," he explained, capturing her hands and kissing her roughly scratched wrists. "I'm not saying you have to be half Enid and half Alexandra any more than I'm saying you should be all Enid or all Alexandra. Just be yourself. That's really all I want you to be. Because I love you for who you are, not who you were . . . or who you're trying to be."

"Oh, Noah." She twined her fingers in his hair and pulled his mouth to hers. When Alexandra broke away, there was no longer a doubt in her mind about anything.

Surf's Up at Sweet Valley

Check out **Sweet Valley Online** when you're surfing the Internet! It is *the* place to get the scoop on what's happening with your favorite twins, Jessica and Elizabeth Wakefield, and the gang at Sweet Valley. The official site features:

Sneak Peeks
Be the first to know all the juicy details of upcoming books!

Hot News
All the latest and greatest Sweet Valley news including special promotions and contests.

Meet Francine Pascal
Find out about Sweet Valley's creator and send her a letter by e-mail!

Mailing List
Sign up for Sweet Valley e-mail updates and give us your feedback!

Bookshelf
A handy reference to the World of Sweet Valley.

★ ★

Check out Sweet Valley Online today!

http://www.sweetvalley.com